FROM THE AUTHOR OF *A SCARCITY OF CONDORS*

A Plump of Woodcocks

ANOTHER COMPENDIUM OF LOVE

SUANNE LAQUEUR

Suanne Laqueur/Cathedral Rock Press
Somers, New York
www.suannelaqueurwrites.com

A Plump of Woodcocks/ Suanne Laqueur. — 1st ed.
ISBN: 978-1-7345518-5-3

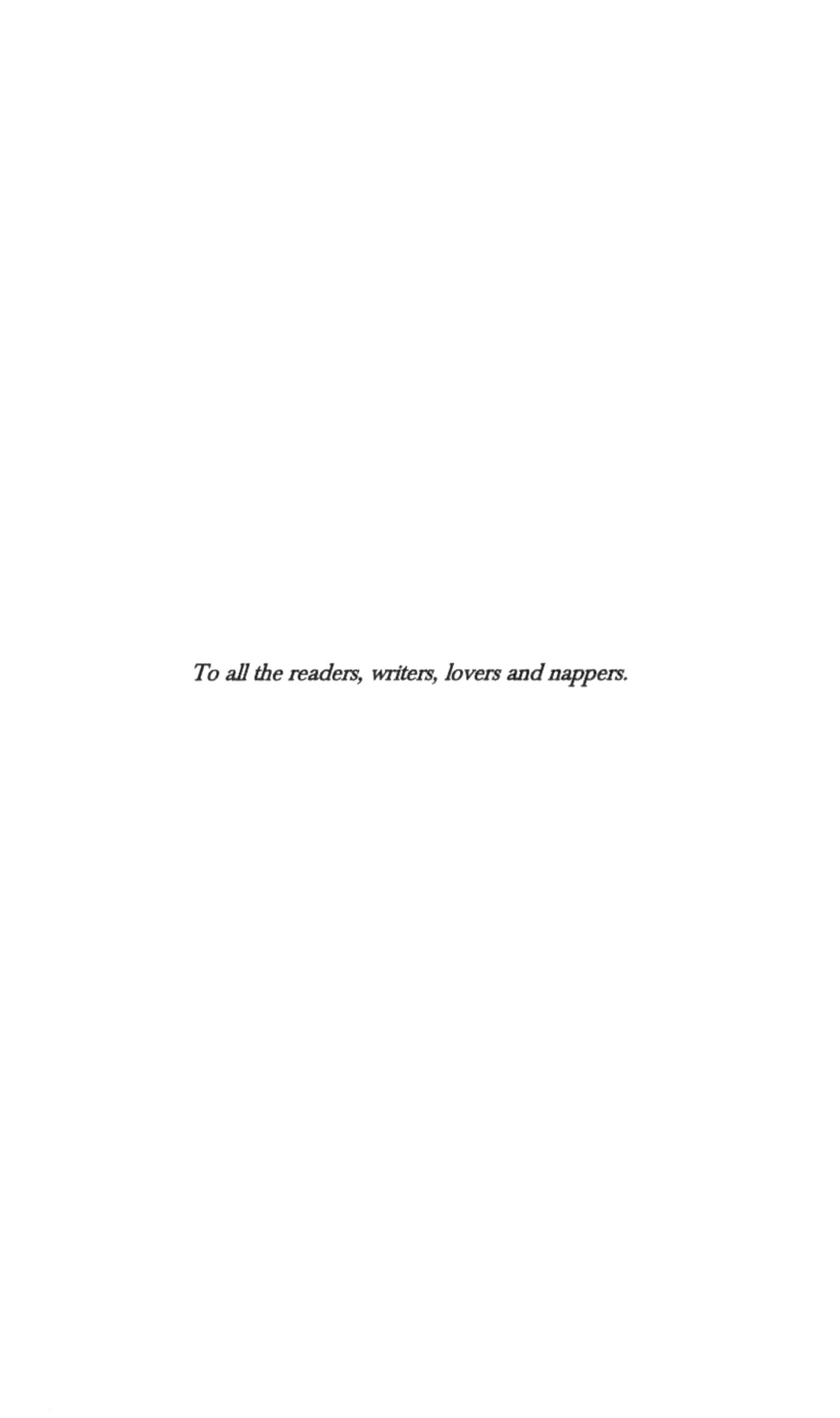

To all the readers, writers, lovers and nappers.

Introduction

SO THIS IS ANOTHER fuckton of gratuitous boning with the *Venery* boys.

That's it, that's the intro. If you're new here, you've been warned. This is pure, shameless smut. It doesn't fit anywhere or take the place of anything in the *Venery* novels. It just is what it is. Smut for smut's sake. No plot, just penis.

If you're old here, welcome back and thank you for taking one for the team.

Before we get to it, I have a brief disclaimer regarding the chapters entitled "Come Back," "Baja La Cabeza" and "Stardust": I DON'T KNOW.

I don't know what happened, but I swear on my children's heads, Stef is all right. He's not going to die. He's going to be fine. I promise.

Don't look at me like that. I mean it. Sheesh, I'm evil to my characters but I'm not cruel.

Fine, I'm a little cruel. But Stef's going to be okay. I *like* him. Jav needs him. The world needs him.

Enjoy.
–SLQR

A Plump of Woodcocks

WESTLING

One of the hardest things about Condors was writing a gay couple that wasn't Jav and Stef. I tried. It helped that both Tej and Jude were definitively gay, had no issue being gay, weren't ever interested in women and needed no physical or psychological training wheels in the bedroom.

I only have two cut scenes of theirs to share. I didn't have to write a lot of back matter to pin their characters down. Tej in particular hit the ground running—every scene with him went from notebook to final draft almost verbatim. From the moment he showed up at the bar, he was quite the force to be reckoned with. Here's how it went down before Jude woke up to an empty bed and an orange. —SLQR

"WHAT ARE YOU LAUGHING AT?" Jude said, torn because he wanted to kiss but wanted to stare at the shape of Tej's smile, too.

"Ever have one of those days that's so bad, instead of trying to turn it around, you go all in and attempt to make it worse?"

"Pretend I have."

"That's what I was doing when I walked over to your booth."

"Yeah?"

"I had a shit day. Everything that could go wrong went wrong. And I saw you sitting in that booth and thought, 'Now there's a guy I'd like to see bent over my bed. I think I'll try to pick him up. End the day on a truly humiliating note.'"

Jude slid his hands down Tej's back and tucked his fingertips beneath the waist of his jeans. "Go back to the bent over your bed part?"

"Well." Tej smiled at the floor. "That was my dick's reaction. I'm cool if you want to top."

Jude wormed one hand a little further down the back of Tej's pants and stroked a finger along his crack. "Well, I was hoping you would top."

Which is kind of a thing, he thought. *A thing I'll think about later. Maybe.*

Now Tej's gaze circled the ceiling, his smile bewildered and beautiful. "This is not happening."

"What?"

"I still can't believe I got the prince consort of Sweden to come home with me." His palms ran warm up the sides of Jude's neck and they kissed again, holding each other's heads.

Get in me, Jude thought, groaning through the slide of Tej's tongue. *Get in here with me and fuck my brains out. You be the brains of the operation and make sense of this shit.*

You seem like a smart guy, as well as gorgeous.

Figure me out.

Please.

He was still wearing his glasses, but when he went to take them off, Tej stopped him. "No. Leave those."

"Why?"

"Because they're fucking hot. Jesus, think I walked over to your booth because you had nice hands? Shut up and kiss me."

Who are you, Jude thought, as Tej's mouth turned and tilted, fitting precisely into his. He pulled Jude's shirt off, then his lips ran hot and shaking along Jude's throat and collarbones, inhaling deep and almost purring on the exhale.

"Man, you kiss crazy," Jude said hoarsely.

"Don't lick your lips like that."

"Don't tell me not to." He unbuttoned Tej's shirt and peeled it off his arms, hungry for smooth, dark skin. Mouth watering for the mat of short, fine hairs on Tej's chest and the whorl around his belly button that tapered into a tight line. A grunt in his chest as Tej unbuttoned and unzipped Jude's jeans, slid a hand inside and found his cock.

"And the night just got even better," Tej said.

"How about that?"

"What other secret weapons are you hiding from me?"

"Take the rest of my clothes off and see."

"About time. Been wanting to get you naked all night."

They kissed open-eyed to the tumble of shoes heeled off and kicked aside. The soft flop of denim, flannel and wool falling to the floor. Belt buckles clinking. Loose change jangling. Each shoulder supporting a steadying hand while the last sock was stripped off. Naked, they moved almost tentatively back together, then with a jolt they were kissing hard, biting and grinding and stroking.

"Before I bend you over my bed," Tej said between panting breaths, "is anything off the table?"

"Not really. Just be nice to me."

Tej startled within his skin. His head drew back, looking at Jude sideways.

"What?" Jude said.

"That's something you can ask for?"

"What do you mean?"

"'Be nice to me.' You just, like, request it?"

Jude smiled and touched Tej's lips. "Sure."

"No, really. This is a thing?"

"Yeah."

"Huh." Tej looked away, brows pulled tight. "I never got that memo."

"Try it."

He looked back. "Be nice to me?"

Jude closed his hand around Tej's erection and circled the damp tip with his thumb. "Okay. But remember you asked."

Now Tej reached up and slid Jude's glasses off. Jude shivered, as if a final piece of clothing were being stripped away.

"Can you see without these?" Tej asked, folding the earpieces down.

"Barely."

"Can you see I'm putting them down on this table here? Right by the door?"

"I should be able to grope my way back to them."

"I'll help guide."

"That's nice of you."

"You asked, remember?"

"Mm. You have condoms?"

"No, I don't have any condoms, said no gay man ever." He gave Jude's head a light swat. "Ask me if I have lube and I'll have to throw you out."

"Got lube?"

Tej shoved him toward the door, reached down to pick up Jude's jeans and pegged them after. "Bye. It's been swell."

Jude stumbled back, threw up a farewell hand and, clutching his pants, turned to make a show of opening the door.

"Don't move," Tej said. "Stay just like that."

Nude, a hand on the doorknob, Jude looked back over his

shoulder, the heady power of his own sex appeal like a battle cry in his veins.

Come and get it, hotshot.

"I said don't move," Tej said. "I want a good look at that ass before I ..."

Jude raised his eyebrows.

"Nicely fuck the shit out of it," he finished.

Jude stared, high on knowing if he merely cracked the door, Tej would be on his knees.

"Whatever you're smiling about," Tej said, coming toward him, "don't stop." He kissed Jude, a hand tight in his hair, tongue going deep. The other hand took the jeans and flung them away. "Now be nice and come with me."

"Say please."

"Please hurry. I only have all night."

In a gesture both commanding and tender, he took Jude's hand and led him down a hall to his room. Once there, he turned and walked backward, drawing Jude toward the bed a few steps.

"This is happening?"

Smiling, Jude nodded. "About to."

Tej moved behind him, put hands on Jude's shoulders and gently moved him toward the corner of the mattress. His palms slid, warm and dry, down Jude's sides, glided across his stomach and up his chest, pressing flat on his heart. And he held him. Through one huge inhale and a slow, trembling exhale, his breath ruffling the back of Jude's neck. His hard cock nestled against Jude's butt.

Jude held still.

Tej kissed his nape. "All right?"

"Mm."

"It's okay if you change your mind."

"I'm not." Jude leaned back, loving the warm, strong pressure all along the rear plane of his body. "I'm just enjoying feeling better."

And I'm digging this be-nice-to-me thing.

He didn't think it was possible, but Tej moved a little closer, held him a little harder. "It'll be all right," he said. "Everything will work out, I promise."

Jude nodded, believing him.

"Just breathe with me."

Long, magic waves of inhales and exhales. Jude closed his eyes, let his head tip back and rest on Tej's shoulder, which was at the perfect height to cradle him. "You feel good."

Tej swayed the tiniest bit, rocking them foot to foot. "Take your time," he said softly. "When you're ready."

Jude ran fingertips across his stomach and over his ribs, then tucked them beneath Tej's broad palms. He drew another breath, wanting to feel the expand and contract of skin and bone and muscle match his. "Almost," he said.

Tej folded fingers around Jude's and held him. "I'll wait."

"This is nice."

"Well, you requested nice." Tej tucked his chin on Jude's shoulder, looking down the plane of his body. "Your skin is crazy." He let go Jude's hands and ran his fingertips up and down. "You don't have a mark on you."

"Mark?"

"I mean, you don't have ink."

"Was never into tattoos."

"You don't need them. You're perfect just like this. Don't mess with it." He kissed Jude's neck, slow and hot and deliberate. "You're fucking perfect, man."

"You're so hard," Jude whispered.

"Yeah. And it's yours if you want it."

"I do. Soon."

"When you're ready for my cock, you bend over for me."

Jude moaned, prickling and melting, going from rock-hard to platinum.

"It's all right." Tej's voice was softer than rain. "When you're ready, it's gonna feel so good."

Jude trembled. Leaned. One palm touched the mattress, folded to an elbow, like a camel settling to the desert sands. His other elbow went down. He reached for a pillow to tuck under his chest.

"Oh, man," Tej whispered, stroking the small of Jude's back. "I can't believe I got you home."

"Me neither." Jude closed his eyes and stepped off the edge of himself. "Now be a nice guy and fuck me."

A rumble beneath his bare feet as Tej dropped to his knees and ran his mouth up the backs of Jude's legs. Before Jude could take a breath, Tej's tongue was on him. Sliding, darting, flicking. Agonizingly fast. Unbearably slow. Rimming Jude within an inch of his life. Then his fingers joined in, helped along with spit and lube until Jude was clinging to the slippery edge of the world, open and panting and craving to be filled up.

"Want this ass so bad," Tej said, breathing hard.

Jude tucked his chin on his shoulder, looking back as much as he could. "You need to fuck me yesterday."

"Put your head down." Tej's palm wide and warm on Jude's temple, pressing him into the pillow. "Relax for me. Let everything go."

His touch was velvet with an edge of callused skin, running up and down Jude's back and sides, curving around his cheeks and spreading him.

"Whole time we were talking tonight, my mouth was watering. Thinking about you like this. Bent over my bed. Getting you spread open and slicked up. Waiting for you to say you were ready."

The tip of Tej's dick touched him. Just pressed and held still through one long breath. Tej reached for Jude's clenched fists.

"Let go your hands." Gently he loosened the fingers. "I want everything open. That's it."

Jude's palms quivered against the sheets. It took several inhales and exhales to make them rest flat. The whole time, Tej held still against him. The consistent pressure skilled and precise. Waiting.

"I could come just like this," he said.

"You better not."

"Shh ..." Tej's hands slid down his back. His thumbs spread Jude wider, then his cock breached, fitting into the space he'd opened up.

A noise tumbled out of Jude's throat. Some primordial groan of fuck-me desperation, edged with ecstasy.

"Oh, baby, that's good," Tej whispered.

He moved slower than the stars across the sky, bit by bit, breath by breath, sliding into Jude's ass.

"It's so good going into you."

Jude burrowed his head down into softness as he was filled up inch by inch with hot, hard need. He closed his eyes and felt his body move out of the way, the complex aching pleasure making the small of his back pull apart sideways, while the vertebra in his spine stretched long. Every muscle, sinew, fiber and cell backing away from Tej while coyly crooking a finger and beckoning, *Come in.*

Come in more. All the way in. More. Further. Deeper.

"God, look how you're taking it. You're so good."

Jude sighed as Tej came down on him, the weight of his chest and belly fitting into the landscape of Jude's back. His hands running along Jude's arms and twining with his fingers.

"Jesus, you're a dream of a fuck," he murmured.

"Yeah?"

"Never had it so easy like this. Like your ass was made for me."

"Bet you say that to all the boys."

"No," Tej said, rubbing his forehead against Jude's temple. "I don't."

And Jude believed him. He couldn't twist back far enough to kiss, but he opened his mouth and let Tej's tongue trace his lips and teeth.

"Am I hurting you?"

"No."

Tej stroked Jude's hair. "Don't tell me what you think I want to hear. I'll stop whenever you need to."

"Don't stop. Just fuck me like you're doing."

Tej moved into him, then dragged back slow. "I can't take it."

"I can take all of it."

"Christ." The bite of ten fingernails in Jude's shoulder blades. "You can't say shit like that."

"Why not?"

"Because it'll make me come in two seconds."

Suffused with power, Jude licked his lips and put a little more arch in his spine, getting his hips up to meet Tej's next thrust and bury it. "Keep doing it like that."

Tej straightened up. "Spread your legs a little more. That's it." His fingers began to press and stretch the skin around Jude's hole. Getting all the involuntary clench to calm down and relax, getting Jude to stay open and easy. Under this skilled, expert pressure, the burn of the breach lowered to a deep heat, until Jude could feel every slow stroke behind his eyes.

"Whatever you're doing, don't stop," he whispered.

But Tej shuddered still and exhaled, his body trembling. "I'm gonna lose it."

"It's so good," Jude said softly.

"Feeling better?"

He chuckled. "Yeah. A lot better."

Tej pulled back and pushed in again. Out and in. Then stilled once more. "I'm right on the edge, this is ridiculous."

"Let me get on top of you," Jude said, rocking back on him a little and pushing up on his arms.

Tej lay down and Jude crawled up his body, planting his knees on either side. He slicked Tej up more and guided him carefully in. Then poured lube into Tej's palm and guided it to his cock. "What I do, you do. Follow how I move."

Tej's hand and Jude's body rose and fell together. Cautiously. Trying it out. Finding a rhythm.

"Feel good?" Tej said.

"Use both hands."

"Like this?"

"Yeah, that's good." Jude moved up along Tej's length, then sank down again as his cock squeezed through Tej's slippery grip. "That's real good."

I used to fuck Feño like this.

He leaned back on his hands and let his head fall toward his shoulder blades.

But you're nothing like him.

"God, look at you," Tej said.

Jude clenched down and Tej tightened his fingers, his eyes fluttering closed and teeth dragging over his bottom lip. Jude shifted weight onto one palm, reached the other to run fingertips through the soft hair on Tej's stomach.

"I can't tell where I stop and you begin," Tej murmured.

"Mm."

His eyes opened. "You are too much, man."

Jude smiled down on him, wicked with power. "You asked for it."

"I did. But I didn't think I'd get it like this."

"Like what?"

"Well, I was going to fuck you. But I think I'm the one getting fucked right now."

Jude threw his weight forward and moved faster. Shifting this way. Angling that way. Three fast, hard pumps, then one agonizing slow one that made Tej's eyes roll back in his head.

"Baby, it's so good," he moaned.

You are like Feño, Jude thought. *But better. You're Feño without the fear. You're not hiding a goddamn thing. You'd bend me over a park bench and rim me in broad daylight, and not care who saw.*

"Don't hold back," Jude said. "Just take it right over the edge and come with me now. Okay?"

Tej closed one hand tight around Jude's cock and reached up with the other hand. "Can you get down here to me? Bring your head here." His fingers slid in Jude's hair, his mouth tugged at Jude's bottom lip. "Give me your mouth while you're fucking me."

Jude pushed into Tej's fingers, squeezed hard around hard and sucked soft on his tongue.

"That's it," Tej whispered. "Fuck me out, Jude ..."

"You're making me come."

"I can feel it. You're so fucking tight on my cock right now."

"Give it to me. Come in me. Deep as you can ..."

Tej seized Jude's hips and thrust up hard. The night detonated, Jude's eardrums bulging against Tej's hoarse voice.

"Jesus fuck, gonna fill you up ..."

The hard, pulsing pressure within turned warmer, wetter, sliding into Jude's prostate over and over, until he was pouring onto Tej's stomach and chest. A blizzard of white spots floating past his eyes and through it, Tej baring his teeth like an ancient beast, hissing and moaning obscenities into Jude's open mouth.

And Jude, to his shock, moaned them right back.

"God, I'm gonna fuck you all night," he said. "I'm just getting started on your cock ..."

He sank his hips down one last time and slumped, spent and gasping, his head in the curve of Tej's neck. Tej's body slowed, his palms opened wide and stroked along Jude's sweaty back and sides. Then he seized Jude's head and kissed him hard, laughing and sucking and biting his lips.

"Holy crap, you are an insane lay." His kiss went a little softer, but the words kept coming hard. "I'm gonna wreck your workday tomorrow because you're not getting any sleep tonight. Not in this bed. After I'm done with your ass, you'll be lucky if you remember your name."

"It's Westling," Jude said. "His Royal Highness Daniel Westling."

WAND

"I LOVE YOUR WEIRD as fuck mind," Tej said. "I love your amazing as fuck heart. I love your hot as fuck body. And the fact that I have all those things is just fucked up *as fuck*. Now move. Don't stand between a gay man and his fiber."

Jude grimaced. "That stuff tastes like sawdust."

"But it keeps my ass immaculate. You're welcome." Tej stomped out of the kitchen.

"Thank you," Jude said softly.

"Drink yours," Tej yelled back. "*All* of it."

Jude drank it. He did anything Tej wanted because Tej did things Jude only dreamed of. Saying things like, "Go shower. Inside and out because I have plans to fuck you. Thoroughly."

Jude swallowed. "Okay." Because what was he going to say—*no thank you?*

He could. The whole reason he liked Tej bossing him around was knowing he could say no, and Tej would dial it back, without question or complaint.

"Get on the bed," Tej said, when Jude emerged in a cloud of steam. "Lie on your stomach and wait for me. Don't touch yourself."

The bathroom door closed.

"Okay," Jude said again, running a palm along the swelling beneath the towel around his waist.

"I said, *don't* touch yourself," Tej yelled.

"Son of a bitch."

"Do I need to repeat the instructions?"

"No."

He lay down on his stomach. And waited. His hands not kept to himself. Wondering just what the hell Tej planned to do to him this time. It was impossible to guess. Sometimes Tej advertised a laundry list of obscene intentions, but delivered ardent, tender lovemaking. Other times he coaxed Jude to bed in a mushy, touchy-feely mood, then turned into Wolverine.

When Tej came in, naked and damp, the anticipation turned inside-out, condensing into a tight, whimpering need in Jude's chest.

"Lose the towel and roll over," Tej said, and as Jude did as told, Tej's voice went all soft and stunned. "God, you're so beautiful, I can't stand it."

Jude smiled, thinking it was going to be a lovemaking night after all.

Next thing he knew, Tej had tied his hands to the headboard.

"Well, this escalated quickly," Jude said.

"That feel okay? Comfort-wise, I mean. Not too tight?"

"Um, no?" He flexed his fingers. "It's just a little out of my comfort zone."

"I know." Tej opened his lower drawer and took out a Hitachi wand.

"Oh boy," Jude said slowly. "This is going to suck, isn't it?"

"Probably."

He shook his head, laughing under his breath. "Whatever happens tonight, just get me to work tomorrow."

Tej flicked the toy on. "You can count on me."

He started running the wand along Jude's erection, the vibration bringing all the veins to the surface.

"Holy shit," Jude murmured, feeling like not only was his cock standing straight up, it was mirror-imaged straight toward his feet.

Where were his feet?

He had to glance down to check. They were still at the ends of his legs, but he couldn't feel them.

"Dude, that's insane," he said. With difficulty, because his tongue seemed to be absent as well.

Tej said nothing, only turned the dial up a hair.

His cells humming like a beehive, Jude stared as the tip of his penis started to leak. Like tears. His dick was *crying*. He'd never seen so much pre-come spill out of him. Poised on one elbow, Tej held the wand still, held Jude poised on the edge, and licked the trail away.

"Jesus," Jude hissed through gritted teeth, his pelvis thrusting without his control.

Tej took away both his mouth and the vibration. "Don't. Come."

"Dude, I'm not the one in control here."

"You are. And you don't come until I tell you."

"I'll try."

Tej slithered down to lie between Jude's knees. "Spread your legs for me now." His slicked finger moved along the crack of Jude's ass. "Little more. That's it, baby." His fingertip pressed and stroked. "I know you want to come so bad. Don't yet. Not until I tell you."

As the fingertip worked slowly in, Jude blew out breath after tremendous breath, pulling himself back from the razor-fine precipice of climax. It was exceedingly difficult without his hands to yank at his hair or clench in the sheets or hold onto Tej's head.

"Squeeze around my finger," Tej said. "Tight as you can. Good. Now let go."

Another ferocious exhale and a moan in Jude's throat as he was breached. Strong, soft pressure sliding into him. Easy as pie. Tej withdrew his finger and Jude chased after it.

"Look at you," Tej said.

"More."

"You want more?"

"Please."

The pressure within doubled up and the world wrapped around Jude twice and pulled tight. "Jesus God, I can't ..." He turned his forehead into his straining bicep, not sure whether to laugh or cry.

"You can, baby. You're doing so good."

The fuck is this? Jude thought through the humming buzz in his brain. *I don't like being called baby. I don't like being petted and told I'm a good boy. I don't need praise and encouragement in bed like it's a new skill I'm learning ...*

Slowly Tej started to fuck Jude's ass with his fingers. "Good boy," he said, and Jude melted under the words.

But with him, I fucking love it.

Shaking with the strange desire, wanting to be good—to be better, to be the *best*—he opened up for Tej. A third finger slid into his ass now. Slow and slippery. Curving in and up and massaging in little circles on his prostate. Edging him from inside.

"I love the shape you make around my fingers."

"Fuck," Jude whispered.

"God, I could come just watching you try not to come."

"You're killing me."

"You're so fucking hot. I could do this all night long, I swear."

Jude wet his lips to reply, but his tongue went dry and the words crumbled to fine dust, blowing away with another deep exhale. Tej pressed hard from within and Jude groaned, nearly a sob in his thick chest. An animal sound between pain and pleasure. His mouth watered, needing to suck and lick and taste on something. He found his voice and begged, "Kiss me."

Somehow, Tej scrabbled up while keeping his fingers deep in motion. Now his tongue fucked Jude's mouth, soft and slow. Biting at his lips, taking Jude's breath and replacing it with his own.

"What do you feel?" Jude asked, not even sure what he meant.

"So tight and hot in your ass," Tej whispered. "So smooth and deep inside you. It feels like trust. You know?"

That was what Jude meant. "Baby," fell off his tongue and into Tej's mouth.

"You want to come now?"

"Please."

Tej reached and tugged at the bonds holding Jude's wrists captive, freeing them. "You take the wand. Go ahead. Run it along your cock. Don't touch anything with your other hand. Put it back over your head now. Good boy. Just use the wand. However feels good."

Jude was whimpering now and he didn't care. Writhing and moaning, clenching and torquing through the crackling minutes. Doing what felt good. Doing what Tej told him to do. Without question. And loving it.

Almost grateful for it.

"Come for me," Tej said, sliding back down the mattress. He gathered Jude's cock into his mouth, pushed his fingers deep and fucked him. Thoroughly. Cell by cell. A methodical and systematic loving. *You, cell, are you fucked? Yes? Good. Next? Are you fucked? Excellent. Next ...*

The thrumming head of the wand rested on Jude's lower belly as he spread wide open, knees splayed, hips bucking into the hot, vibrating hole of Tej's mouth. His ass clenched down tight and he both pushed and pulled, trying to pour himself out while drawing

Tej in.

Then he came.

Hard.

For minutes, it seemed.

"God, baby, you're so good," Tej whispered.

Jude gasped for air, lungs burning as if he'd run six miles in sub-zero weather. "I'm not *doing* anything."

Tej wrapped arms around Jude's body and laughed and laughed against his stomach. "Yes, you are."

HOME

But at the end of the day, it's these two. Writing them always feels like coming home. —SLQR

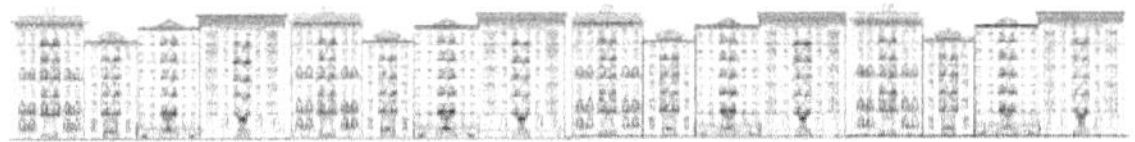

CAN WE GO? Stef texted.

Jav looked around the bar but couldn't see him. He typed back, **Now?**

Now.

Why.

Because work sucked today, this scene is boring, the drinks are too expensive and I just want to go home and fuck my boyfriend.

Heat filled Jav's face, while his stomach curled goofily around *boyfriend.*

Can I finish my costly drink? he typed.

Chug it. I'm walking out. Follow me and you won't regret it.

"I gotta get going," Jav said, slamming the last of his Appleton Estate. "Good to meet you."

"Call me," the woman said, passing him a card.

He held it in his teeth and smiled as he shrugged on his jacket. In the foyer of the bar, he crumpled the card and dropped it in the trashcan. A year ago, he'd never do such a thing. Six *months* ago he wouldn't. Or he'd at least hesitate.

Outside, Stef slouched against the building, hands in his pockets, ankles crossed. In the cold city light, he looked beautiful, but tired. Only one side of his mouth smiled as he pushed off the wall and held his hand out to Jav. "Come on."

The goofy curl in Jav's stomach again as he regarded the outstretched arm. It coiled tight as he slid his fingers between Stef's and they started walking down Ninth Avenue.

Going home so Stef could fuck his boyfriend.

Fuck me like … fuck me? Jav thought. *Or was that just an expression?*

His goofy mood downshifted a little. Six weeks of dating and parts of his brain still couldn't *relax*. Not once had he felt uncomfortable with Stef in bed, or coerced or intimidated, but he couldn't stop being so damn cerebral about sex. Sexual language in particular. Stef threw one provocative F-bomb and Jav immediately examined the fuse to see if it led to his ass.

Take a fucking chill.

"Sorry to be lame," Stef said. "Wednesdays aren't my best social night."

"I get it. No worries."

"I'm beat and I just want you to myself." He hooked an arm around Jav's neck. A four-footed, laughing stumble and a warm buss against Jav's sideburn, which turned icy cold when Stef took his mouth away. He took Jav's hand again and they were quiet as they walked, weaving around and through pedestrians. They passed another gay couple coming north. Four chins gave The Nod and eight eyes took silent inventory.

Brothers, well met.

Hail, brothers.

All is well tonight?

All is well. So may it be with you.

Go in peace and pride.

Be safe.

Jav was at peace tonight, safe in his city, proud to be holding hands with Stef, who was beat and only wanted Jav to himself.

"Oh man," Stef said, yawning. "Sorry."

"You work hard," Jav said.

Stef yawned again, then smiled sheepishly at Jav, his dimple flickering. Jav ruffled his hair, guessing the "go home and fuck my boyfriend" thing would translate to some lazy kissing and touching under the covers. The Five-Minute Frottage, as Stef liked to say. Get in, get off and goodnight.

Jav knew worse ways to finish a Wednesday.

Stef had given him a key to Cushman Row. Rather than put it on his own fob, Jav carried it in his pocket, like a good luck charm. Dopey, but he liked it there. Liked having that ounce of symbolism close at hand. Sitting down and feeling it poke him in the hip. Fishing it out and turning it in the lock of Stef's door. Knowing one of the hinges was wonky so you had to pull up on the knob a little and give it a bump with your shoulder.

"Remind me to fix the damn hinge this week," he said, closing the door with a backward kick of his heel.

The breath punched out of his lungs as Stef lunged and pushed him up against the wall. "Fix the damn hinge this week," he said, before his mouth sank into Jav's.

Wait, this isn't Wednesday.

The thought sloshed side to side as the back of his head rattled against the wall, then rebounded into Stef's kiss.

Whoa. Wait. What?

Stef's warm, soft tongue in his mouth. A metallic clatter of keys and change as Stef's hands pulled Jav's jacket down his arms and threw it aside. Then his hands taking Jav's face, spreading wide across his jaw and ears and pulling him in, tasting like everything good in the world.

"Could fucking kiss you forever," he said, moving Jav's head into the crook of one elbow.

Jav leaned back against Stef's arm, tilted his chin up. Groaned at the hot shaking wet down his throat. Shivered at the fingers now busy at his buttons, one at a time undoing him. Cool air through Jav's open lapels, then Stef caught both his wrists up tight and pressed them to the wall. His kiss went deep as he leaned on Jav's body, his clothes wrinkling and bunching against Jav's bare skin. He was hard in his jeans, rubbing it between Jav's legs. The scent of the cold winter night in his hair as his head bent and he closed his mouth around Jav's nipple and sucked hard. A pinch of pain followed by a warm wet caress, making Jav groan again.

"You're so fucking beautiful." Stef let go of Jav's wrists and grabbed his ass, pulling him in and grinding their erections together. "I can't keep my eyes off you. Can't keep my hands and my mouth off you."

His lips dragged over Jav's ribs, across his stomach. The tip of his tongue in Jav's belly button and now those confident fingers at his belt buckle. Stef's forehead on his skin as he dropped on his knees. The pop of another button, the metallic glide of a zipper. Then he was reaching in, taking out Jav's penis and running his tongue up the hard length and circling the head, which was already leaking, dripping and twitching with need.

"Been wanting this all night." Stef's eyelashes fluttered across his cheekbones. He was closed up tight within himself, humming in his throat, one hand clasped tight around Jav's cock, the other pulling down Jav's pants, tugging them off one foot, then the other.

"God, you taste so fucking good," he said.

"Yeah?" Jav gasped, stunned as always by his lover's fierce, uninhibited delight in going down on him.

"Mm." Stef's eyes opened as he drew back. "I can't believe how perfect you fit in my mouth. I mean all of you. I'm fucking obsessed." The tip of his tongue ran along the underside of Jav's cock and curled around the sweet spot beneath the head. "Never been so orally fixated on someone, I swear."

"Jesus ..."

"I suck you off and I want to be kissing you. I go to kiss you and can't wait to get your dick back in my mouth. I literally can't get enough of you on my tongue. It's fucking ridiculous."

He kissed up Jav's quivering belly and heaving chest. He seized Jav's head and kissed deep. "Come on," he said, taking Jav by the shoulders and backing him toward the bedroom. He sat Jav down at the corner of the mattress, stripped his own clothes off and fell on his knees again. "Lie back now," he said. "I'm gonna make you come harder than you ever came in your life."

"You said that last night."

"I lied."

"God."

Jav planted his feet and pushed his hips up into Stef's mouth, crazed and desperate. Stef curled an arm around his leg, holding it open and pinned with his shoulder, running his teeth in the hollow of Jav's groin, gathering each ball into his mouth, exploring secret, underneath places Jav didn't know existed. He rose and fell over Jav's body like the tide. His mouth was everywhere at once, sucking on Jav's lips, his fingertips, his nipples and his cock, God, the click of his throat as he took Jav all the way down and growled against his belly.

Fuck me, Jav thought. *If this is fucking me, then do it, keep doing it, do it harder and don't stop.*

"Feel good?" Stef whispered.

"I can't even ... say."

"I love doing this to you."

This, Jav thought. He pushed up on his elbows. "Hey."

"What?"

He hesitated, running his hand along Stef's jaw. "You think of this as fucking me?"

"Oh hell yeah." He turned his mouth into Jav's palm. His voice was almost shy as he asked, "Do you?"

"Yeah. I do now. Like I get it now."

"Good." Stef's smile filled his hand. "Now lie down so I can fuck your brains out."

Jav fell back. The breath collapsing out of his lungs, then pulling in sharp as Stef went at him again. "Finch," he whispered.

"Your dick is so good in my mouth," Stef said hoarsely, breathing hard. "Going down on you is a fucking piece of cake."

"I've never been blown like this in my life," Jav said. "I'm not kidding."

"I know," Stef said, his mouth gliding along the shaft and tonguing the slit. "And it's about fucking time."

"Oh my God."

"I could come just watching you. You're so fucking hot when I'm sucking you off." He swallowed Jav down and Jav let out a howl, spreading his legs, bucking up into the warm, wet heat, opening as far as he could reach. Stef's touch slid beneath his balls and the heel of his hand rubbed hard in Jav's crack, then his fingers touched, soft and curious.

"Can I?" he whispered.

"Yeah."

The bedside table drawer opened and closed. "I'll only go in a little," Stef said, flipping open the cap on the lube. "If you don't like it, just say so."

"All right."

"Promise me you'll say so."

"I'll say."

Stef's mouth gathered Jav up again, drew him down deep and let him go slow. "Fucking love this cock," he whispered. "Your whole body makes me insane. I go around all day with a hard-on for you."

"Oh my God, man."

Stef moved up and set his brow against Jav's, while his arm stretched long and heavy on Jav's body, moving between his bowed thighs. He kissed Jav and a slick fingertip pressed against Jav's ass. "I'll go slow. Just breathe with me. Look at me and breathe."

Foreheads and gazes pressed, they breathed together, Stef pressing a little more with every exhale. On the third breath, his fingertip slid inside, soft and snug.

"Oh," Jav whispered.

It fits, he thought. *Just like that?*

Stef kissed him. "All right?"

"Christ."

"Hurt?"

"No."

Stef smiled, the dimple creasing his cheek. "Just weird?"

"Yeah, but ... weird in a good way."

"I'll stop whenever you want."

"What's it feel like to you?"

"Warm. Warm and smooth and so fucking tight. It's like a tight secret."

"Secret?"

"Nobody knows how it feels in you but me."

They kissed, open-mouthed and enormous, while Stef's finger slid gently in and out, a little farther each time. "You're taking it so good," he said against Jav's throat.

Jav peeled open to the night. *It feels good*, he thought, experimentally. *I take it good. I'm good at this.* His hips began to rise up to meet Stef's touch, until Stef was holding still and Jav was moving on him. Playing around with the fullness. Tilting and shifting and finding the place where it went from good to ...

"That is *fucked up*," he murmured behind closed eyes, sawing back and forth on the complex spot of tingling, buzzing madness.

"Need to stop?" Stef said.

"No." He reached for the lube bottle. "Let me feel two now."

Stef slid a second finger into Jav's ass.

"Now do that and fuck me with your mouth." Was that his voice? He barely recognized himself, sprawled out on the bed, legs splayed and forearms crossed over his face, hissing his blunt need into the night.

I'm going crazy, he thought. *I'm going to lose my mind. Am I even here?*

He freed one arm and reached down to find the reassurance of Stef's thick hair, damp at the back of his neck as his head bobbed up and down and around Jav's cock. Hot, wet heat followed by cool, dry air. A hard squeeze then a soft caress. His thick, slick fingers sliding into Jav's ass and rubbing in little circles at what seemed to be the very center of the universe.

"Want to see you come," Stef said. "Want to feel you come with your cock in my mouth and my fingers in your ass."

"Fuck me," Jav whispered. Testing the words, finding they held under his weight and then leaning on them more. "Fuck me, Stef."

"Let me fuck you like this. Feel it in your ass when you come in my mouth."

"More. Give it to me more."

Stef's fingers pressed against the roots of Jav's cock, pulsing power up through the tip into Stef's mouth, looping around again and again until Jav couldn't tell where he stopped and Stef began.

"Baby, fuck me like this," Jav whispered, fearless now. "Feels so good when you fuck me with your mouth."

He clenched around Stef's fingers and within that fevered grip he felt the vision lock into place. He got it. The fingers inside him became Stef's cock. The heaviness in his chest was from Stef's weight on him. The strain of his hips was from Stef holding his legs apart and instead of gasping at the empty air, his mouth was full of Stef's kiss.

This is how we'd make love.

He could see the sculpture of their four limbs. He could feel the small of Stef's back beneath his heels, the solid mass of Stef's body filling his arms, Stef's hard cock filling his ass, pushing Jav to come from within. He could see it. He could feel it. It was a piece of fucking cake and he wanted it in his mouth.

"Like that?" Stef said.

"Yeah, make me come like that," Jav cried through his teeth as the room began to splinter apart.

He came like that. Came in pieces. Came drooling, his chin slick with spit as he poured into Stef's mouth. Came so hard, tears leaked out the corners of his eyes. Stef licked them away, lying on top of Jav now, his kiss enormous in Jav's mouth.

"Just watching that got me off," he said. "I knew it would."

"You came?" Jav said, still catching his breath. "Both your hands were on me, how did you ...?"

"It was like nothing. You started going, your ass got all tight around my fingers and that was it. Blew a load in my lap like a teenager."

"That's some fucking magic."

Stef laughed and kissed him. "God, I can't handle how good it is with you."

"I had no idea it could be like this."

"I'm the only one who's ever made love to you. Do you have *any* idea what that means to me?"

"I do. You are. And it's all I think about. All the time."

"Me too. Everything I do is oriented around getting home and doing this. I walk in the door and I can't get on you fast enough." His weight on top of Jav shifted. "Am I too heavy?"

"No, I love it. I love ... just being under you like this. It's like ... It's safe."

"I know. I love getting through the day and getting home to you and this."

Jav closed his teeth on Stef's lip, then kissed his full, swollen mouth. Licked his tongue, sucked on it a little, then ran his thumb across his smile.

A long staring moment.

"Stef?"

"Yeah?"

"I'm falling in love with you."

Stef exhaled and curled his head into the curve of Jav's neck. He moved on top of him again and his back shuddered as he pulled Jav's legs around his waist. "Put your arms around my neck," he whispered. "Now hold still. Don't fall anymore. Just be right here in love with me."

His arms scooped beneath Jav's body, pulled him close, rocking them side to side a little.

"I didn't know," Jav said.

"Neither did I. I was married and I didn't know."

"Can't believe I found you. It's crazy."

"Man, if I'd known you were out there, I would've never stopped looking."

Jav rubbed his lips along Stef's temple. "You make everything so good."

"It's so easy. Loving you is so fucking easy."

"Piece of cake."

"Yeah. Just keep following me and you'll get both magic and cake."

Jav pressed his face against Stef's, wrapped and tightened his limbs like a knot. "So this is what it's like?"

"This is it."

"It happened?"

"It's happening. You're here."

"I love you." It slipped easily out of his mouth. Just as easily as *fuck me* a few moments ago.

Because it's the same thing.

He ran his hands up and down Stef's back.

We found each other.

"It's crazy," he said to the night.

"I know." Stef held his head on his shoulder, still rocking them. "I'm so in love with it all."

Jav closed his eyes.

He was home.

FLIP

What if 9/11 never happened? I know millions of people have asked themselves that question. From a personal perspective. A political perspective. A socio-economic, religious or philosophical perspective. We've all imagined alternate scenarios. No doubt Jav has.

Stef, too ...
—SLQR

"YOU'RE HOME?" FLIP SAID.

"I am," Jav said. "I thought you were at the wedding."

"I am."

"What, you're calling me from the ceremony?"

"No, the reception."

"Ah. Can I get the visual, please?"

"Visual?"

"Indoor? Outdoor? Black tie? White tie?"

"Indoor but with a big terrace overlooking the ocean, strung with about a billion Christmas lights in the trees. Not black tie but dressy. Waiters circling with trays—Oh hello, what's this you got?

Mini quiche lorraine. Love it, thank you."

"Feels like I'm there," Jav said.

"I fucking wish," Flip said around a mouthful. "If you were here, we wouldn't be here."

"Where would we be?"

"I don't know. Far away. Alone. Finally."

"We've been alone before."

"Not with me knowing how your tongue feels in my mouth. That's a whole different kind of alone."

"True," Jav said.

"What are you doing home on Friday night? I thought for sure you'd have a date."

"If you were sure, why'd you call?"

Flip's laughed curled around Jav's ear like a caressing fingertip. "To see if you'd pick up. I don't know escort etiquette, but I imagine high on the list is you don't break the spell of attention to take calls from musicians."

"Number one rule. But I'd take yours."

"Bull to the shit, you would."

"I might. Sneak to the men's room to see what you wanted."

"What if I said, 'I want you. Break the date, walk out. Leave the money and talk to me because your voice gives me a hard-on'?"

"Well ..." Jav faked a resigned sigh as he adjusted his stirring erection. "Truth be told, I am on a date. And I am in the men's room, sneaking your call. And considering breaking, walking and leaving."

"You are so full of shit."

"Yeah. I am. So ..."

"So."

"How was the wedding?"

"I don't want to make small talk. What did you do today? Tell me everything."

"Just small things."

"Tell me one."

"I got up, I ran."

"What else? Tell me a story."

Jav hesitated, then closed his eyes and confessed. "I took a shower, rubbed one out and thought about you."

Flip's laugh punched his ear now, a full-throated crow. "*That's* what I'm talking about."

"I like a story with a happy ending."

"I told the same one this afternoon."

"Shut up."

"If it weren't for the time difference, it would've totally counted as fooling around. Anyway. What then?"

"I worked. I thought about you. I had lunch. I wrote a little. I thought about you. That's my day, man. Working and thinking about you, which means not a whole lot of work got done."

"What were you thinking?"

"I don't know. Things." A flustered shyness took Jav by the tongue. He got up from the couch and paced, trying to distance it. Yet kind of digging the warm, goofy rush in his face and chest.

"Tell me one thing."

"Just ... seeing you again. Picturing it like three different ways. Meeting you at the airport. Or you taking a cab to my place. Or me cabbing up to your place."

"One and three are out," Flip said. "Airport is too full of gawking strangers. My place is too close to gawking family members, plus Talin has his own key. I'll cab to your place. If you don't mind, I mean."

"It's the opposite of minding."

"My fantasy was getting back to my hotel room tonight to find you in it."

"That's a good one. I had another scenario of flying to Cali to surprise you, only to get there and find you'd flown back to New York to surprise me."

"Dude, that's the worst fantasy I've heard in my life. *How* much do you make an hour?"

"Hey, I get paid to fulfill women's fantasies, not script them."

"You do get paid, yes."

A long beat of silence.

Jav swallowed hard. "I confess I've also been wondering if my line of work was going to be a problem with ... us."

"Well," Flip said slowly. "If you had male clients, maybe. But it's kind of unreasonable to ask a dude to abandon his lucrative livelihood when you haven't even gone on, like, an actual date."

"True."

"But if you want to know how I feel about it ...?"

"Kind of. Yes. Tell me."

"I'm equal parts fascinated and ... confused. I guess. Weird how as a man, I'm ingrained to look at a male escort and be admiring and envious. You know? Think, *Wow, that's the life. Paid to fuck. All the benefits, none of the hassle. Good on you, mate.* But I know now what led you to that life. I know a little more about what keeps you in it. I know this whole other side to you that I like to pretend your clients don't."

"You don't have to pretend," Jav said. "They don't. Barely anyone does. Russ, to an extent. Now you."

"It just puts a bittersweet spin on it. The idea of you selling yourself doesn't seem so glamorous anymore. You know?"

"Yeah."

"Not to be poetic but I think you're a priceless kind of guy."

Jav laughed softly, because he couldn't think of anything to say.

"Anyway," Flip said, his voice rising a little. "I'm cool if you want to put a pin it. Future conversation, depending how things go. Let's get back to bad fantasies. What are you wearing?"

"I miss you," Jav blurted.

Flip's breath shook over the line. "Yeah, man, I miss you too."

"I've been wearing your hat."

"Yeah?"

"When I write."

"Does it give you any good ideas?"

"The kind that go in the shower, not on paper."

"Oh, man. Remind me, what the fuck am I doing in California?"

"I don't know but I can't wait for you to get back."

"Neither can I. I want to make love so bad."

Jav's chest got all thick and tight. Equal parts curiosity and trepidation. "I've never ... been with a guy."

"At all? Nothing?"

"My cousin kissed me twenty years ago. I liked it. A lot. But it cost me everything. Literally everything. In the time since, I got hired by couples twice. The first time, the guy went nowhere near me and the second time, the guy went near me and I started to like it. Then I freaked out."

"I see."

"Kissing and a little bit of freaked-out touching. That's my experience."

"I kind of love that," Flip said, his voice velvet.

"Why?"

"Well, the thought of showing you something you've never experienced before doesn't exactly suck."

"Oh."

"*Properly* experienced. Without all the dire consequences."

"Being with a guy consequence-free," Jav said. "Imagine that."

"Let's be honest, you exude sexual confidence, but I know now it's your professional side. Your game face, your armor, whatever. Underneath is the stuff you're telling me right now. It's the hungry but uncertain you. The vulnerable you."

"Newsflash: I'm not good with vulnerability."

"Maybe. Yet here you are, telling me scary shit from the other side of your coin. It's large, man. I might even file it under *priceless*."

"I handle being vulnerable by asking a lot of questions. Sometimes a lot of idiotic questions. Because I don't like change. Or rather, I'm okay with change, I just don't like sudden change. I don't like surprises. I don't like looking stupid or ..."

"Image is kind of a thing with you."

"Yeah. So bear with me. When I'm in an unknown situation, I throw a lot of information at it."

"Ask me anything," Flip said. "It would bother me more if you didn't."

"So, when you said, 'I want to make love' ... What does that mean to you?"

"Mean?"

"Like, when you close your eyes and think about me. Us. Making love. What do you see?"

"I see ..." He trailed off, then laughed a little. "Shit, I got shy all of a sudden."

"Tell me."

"God your voice makes me crazy. Um. Let me think. I need to move somewhere else because there's no hiding what's going on below my belt now."

"Sorry."

"The hell you are. Hold on."

"Where are you going?"

"Like, down some stairs from the terrace. Out on this grassy kind of bluff. I feel like a Ralph Lauren ad. Very cool sunset tonight, by the way. All right." He exhaled long. "I see a lot of things when I close my eyes, but I don't want to freak you out."

"You won't. I just want to know."

"I want to lie down with you. On your bed. With nowhere else to go. Just be alone together. You and me and time. But before that ..." He trailed off again.

"What?" Jav said. "You're laughing."

"I want to go back to your kitchen," Flip said. "I want to sit on the counter with you standing between my knees. I want to start there. Start over. With no interruptions or dire consequences this time."

"Jesus Christ, I want that too."

"Honestly, man, I think about the kitchen more than I think about being in bed with you."

"Me too. I ..." Speechless under a widening grin, Jav ran a hand along his kitchen countertop.

"You're laughing now," Flip said. "Tell me."

"Nothing. Just that I stand at my counter and pretend you're there all the time. It's ridiculous."

"You don't."

"I do. I put my hands far apart on the counter, I drop my head and pretend it's on your shoulder. I'm doing it right now. Don't laugh at me."

"I'm only laughing because last night, I sat on the bathroom vanity and pretended."

"Shut up."

"I swear. Sitting on the vanity in the dark bathroom holding an armful of pillows. Pretending I was kissing the shit out of you."

"Oh my God." Jav's head rolled side to side, conjuring up a hard shoulder, wanting it with every atom.

"So yeah, I want the kitchen back," Flip said. "Then maybe we can go lie down."

"Okay."

"And ... Damn, I've never talked like this to a guy, I'm getting all shy again."

"You haven't?"

"No. Now that I think about it, whenever I've hooked up with a guy, it was never very … verbal. You know? Never a slow burn like this. It was immediate and in the moment, with not much discussion."

"Spontaneous."

"Yeah. So you bear with me here. This is vulnerable shit."

"I know. My heart's pounding."

"I want to lie down with you. And eventually I want us to take our clothes off. Because your body … your body is so fucking beautiful. It's been filling up my eyes and making my hands ache for months. I don't know how the hell I walked away from it the other night."

"I don't know how the hell I let you out the door."

"I must've gone temporarily straight."

"That's obviously what happened."

"Now I just want to lie down next to your body and hold it for like an hour. If your heart's pounding, I want to feel it against me. If you're shaking, I want to feel that. If you're hard, I want to feel that."

Jav slid down the cabinet doors to sit on the floor. "I'm all those things right now."

"Me too."

"I'm so hard for you."

"The way your voice shook when you said that is incredible."

"Jesus."

"I want to kiss. And touch. I want to touch each other until we come. I want to feel that against me too. I want to feel you come in my hands."

Jav closed his eyes, dying. "Oh fuck, man."

"That's what I see. And yeah, I call it making love. Because this isn't a hook-up to me. This isn't a spontaneous, in the moment thing. This has a past. And a present. And a future."

"I wish you were here." The words were bricks in Jav's throat. He felt like crying, he wanted so badly.

"Me too," Flip said. "It hurts I want to be there so bad right now."

"What else do you think about?"

"Everything. Touching you everywhere. Kissing you everywhere. Making you feel good. Making you come in a way you never have before. Making ... making sex new to you. Not business but pleasure. You know?"

"Yeah. I mean no. But I want to know."

"That's what I want."

Jav dug his fingers into his hair, pulled hard enough to hurt and clear his aching thoughts. "Do you think about ... I mean, do you want to ..."

Flip chuckled. "Javi, my man, are you trying to ask me who's going to top?"

Fiery hot blood swept across Jav's face. "Kind of."

"It doesn't matter to me. When I close my eyes and ... dream, fantasize, whatever, my mind goes everywhere. Me inside you, you inside me, neither of us inside either of us. It's just whatever we want to do together. You don't like something, you tell me. If I don't like something, I tell you. Can we lay down those ground rules?"

"Okay."

"When you get down to it, all I want is for us to lie naked in bed and tell each other things. Show each other things."

"Okay. But you think about being inside me?"

"Jesus, yes. And you in me."

"Is it good?"

Flip gave a little groan. "Rude bwoy, sometimes I come so hard thinking about it."

"Come home," Jav said. Begged.

"Javi, baby, I can't wait."

"I'm so hard, waiting here for you ..."

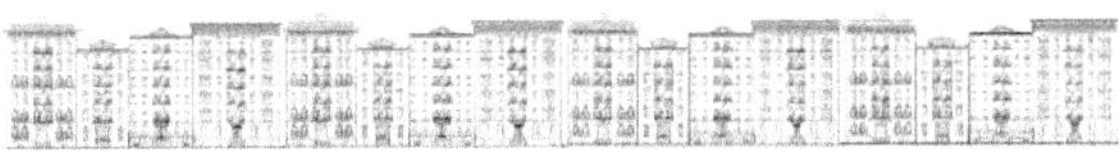

STEF LOOKED UP FROM the paper and stared at a blank spot on the wall. His fingers shook, wanting to crush and crumple the pages, but then Jav would know they'd been touched.

"Fuck," he muttered, flipping the stapled wedge of papers back to the first page and tossing it down. He scrubbed hard at his face, upset and guilty. It was his own damn fault. Jav was away at a signing and Stef was home alone. Bored to death. Feeling a little abandoned and in a weird, needy mood. So he snooped the desk drawers where Jav kept his old work. Not even looking for anything specific, just looking for ... something.

You snoop, you suffer.

He rubbed a corner of the cheap printer paper, trying to smooth out the curl of age. The page footers were date stamped 2002. This pain was old. No, not old—it was venerable.

A poignant, haunting scene, he mused, imagining himself reviewing the tiny work. *Filled with the venerable pain of an alternate ending ...*

He crossed his arms over his heart, leaned far back in the chair and sighed. "Fuckity fuck."

He shouldn't be surprised Jav wrote it. He wasn't. Who in the world *didn't* imagine an alternate ending to 9/11, with four flights landing when and where they were supposed to? Business finished. Stories continued. Life uninterrupted.

Absolutely no wonder Jav scripted this fantasy, giving him and Flip Trueblood their alternate ending. Writing them through the frustration of a temporary, toe-curlingly delicious delay. Probably if Stef snooped more, he'd find other scenes. Flip coming back, cabbing to Jav's place on St. Nicholas Avenue, where they'd be lying down in bed within minutes. Holding each other for hours. Not emerging from the building for days. They'd get a September 15th, 16th, 17th and all the weeks, months and years after.

Flip would be Jav's first male lover, not Stef.

Probably his only male lover.

Shit, that would even eliminate Alex Penda.

Without 9/11, Jav might've never *seen* Alex again. Ever. Jav would still get the call telling him his sister had died and he was the guardian of her son, but Jav and Flip would've gone together, as a couple, to bring Ari back into their lives.

And Ari wouldn't have met Deane. He wouldn't know Roger Lark was his father. None of that soap opera would've come to light.

Jesus, what a butterfly effect. Everything would've gone differently. For so many people.

And we wouldn't have met, Stef thought. *No way, no how. Javi's notebooks and papers wouldn't be in my desk for me to rifle through. I'd have a whole other life with someone else.*

Who would that have been?

Maybe I would've hooked up with Trelawney Lark during the Poughkeepsie women's shelter exhibition. Maybe Deb Cenk and I would be together. I might be shacked up with Thomas, for fuck's sake. Who knows? I wouldn't know what I was missing.

I'd read Client Privilege *but I'd never know the author was my fucking soul mate. I'd have no idea we were meant to be together.*

How many people are walking around with the wrong mate because of a tragedy?

How many are walking around with the right mate for the same reason?

Was he supposed to be grateful? It felt downright shitty to lend any kind of gratitude or silver lining to 9/11. What inhumane asshole looked back on the past decade and thought, "Well, thank *God* for September Eleventh ..."

He glanced up at the bulletin board over the desk. Once upon a time, it only contained his little pinnings and Post-its and ephemera. Now Jav's notes and clippings and inspirations were layered over and under and in between. Including a printed postcard from PostSecret.com. A sketch of billowing smoke over the World Trade Center and the hand-lettered confession: *Everyone who knew me before 9/11 believes I'm dead.*

Stef's gaze moved over to the bookshelves, stopping at the neat, proud stack of Jav's books. The fat spine of *The Trade*, the novel Jav sussed out from the postcard. A story of 9/11 being the beginning of a life, rather than an end. An opportunity to escape, instead of a permanent cage of grief and pain.

Next to *The Trade* was the dark blue spine of *The Voyages of Trueblood Cay.* Stef blinked at it a few times, then pushed back from the desk and walked over to take it down. This was his own personal copy, lovingly inscribed by Jav. Several pages were dog-eared, others had underlined passages or little notes in the margin. Stef didn't just read a book, he marked it like a lover. He devoured it, leaving a trail of greasy fingerprints, crumbs and coffee splatters.

But more than his personal copy, this was *his* book. Jav said so.

"C'mon, we know it's Flip's book," Stef had replied.

"The idea came from him," Jav said. "He gave it a face and a name and a concept. But the *book* ... That's all you. The story didn't come together until after I met you. I finally stopped fooling around in my head and *wrote* it when I was falling in love with you. I finished it when I was living with you, with your ring on my finger and a finch tattooed on my neck. When gelang stopped being a private joke and started being a ... a *thing.*

"Without you, *Trueblood* would still be an idea I didn't take seriously. It's a story because of you. Because of us." Jav pushed the book against Stef's chest. "It's not Flip's book. It's yours."

Stef went to the front, looking at his name in the dedication. He went to the acknowledgments at the back and found his name again. His thumb fanned the pages, his eyes catching the name Fen over and over. He was all over this book. His career lived in its plot. The story was woven with his life, his work, his family and his name. His eyes and hair, his tattoos, his rings. Jav's love for him in every word.

Stef stopped, backtracked, looking for a specific scene.

> *"I'm sorry."*
>
> *Trueblood held Fen tight. "It's forgiven. It all happened so you could be with me. Which means I need to be fucking worth it."*
>
> *Everything was pouring out of Fen's eyes and he couldn't answer.*
>
> *Trueblood went on talking. "It also means what happened is mine to protect ..."*

Stef closed the book around his finger and looked up with a long exhale. "That's really it, isn't it?" he asked the postcard on the bulletin board.

It all happened so you could be with me.

Which means I need to be fucking worth it and it's mine to protect.

He slid the book back on its shelf. He smoothed the pages of the little story and put it carefully back where he found it.

Grateful beyond words, he closed the desk drawer.

TWISTED

In the spring, Stef took on a new case.

A horrible case.

A case that made Ronnie Danvers reassign all of Stef's other clients, made Frank Stein insist Stef make and keep a standing, weekly appointment with him, and made a new prescription bottle of Xanax show up in the medicine cabinet.

"This is worse than the Mengele Ring?" Jav asked.

Stef nodded, and even if he'd been able to share the details with Jav, Jav would've refused them. He decided from the start, he'd forbid the case to enter their house. It could squat outside the door to its vile heart's content, but it could not come in.

There was no discussion. Jav just started doing things, making little changes to keep Stef from having to do anything when he got home from work. By five o'clock, Jav's laptop was closed and the desk lamp turned off. Most of the lights were turned off and candles lit on the coffee table and the kitchen counter. The TV was dark, the radio silenced, Roman walked. Something simple was on the stove or in the oven, or takeout ordered and kept warm. Beer was always in the fridge. Mallomars at the ready. Little things that let Stef arrive at an oasis of quiet, nourishing calm.

Home.

What Jav still couldn't do was figure out which nights Stef needed to be left alone with himself, and which nights he needed to be fucked back to himself. And Stef, the paragon of a self-aware, transparent open book, still struggled to communicate that twisted need.

"It's not twisted," Jav said.

"To me it is. I mean, to the deep-down, subconscious, un-nuanced me."

Jav tried to anticipate the need, but he hated making an aggressive move only to be rebuffed. He hated more giving Stef space and finding out later he wanted aggression.

"What about a code word?" Jav asked. "Or a code gesture? I don't know, like, text 'twisted' to me. Or peel the label off your beer bottle and that's the signal for me to fuck the hell out of you."

"That was like a thing in college," Stef said. "Wasn't it?"

"What? Hell Fucking 101?"

"No, the label thing. If you saw someone peeling the label off their beer, it meant they were horny."

"Maybe at Skidmore. We did things differently at CCNY. Anyway, the point is ... whatever point I was making."

"I guess let's try the code word thing. Twisted. Whatever."

He sounded pissy about it, but Jav let it go. Until this unspeakably horrible case was over—or at least under manageable control, because Jav knew by now these things were rarely *over*—he'd pick his battles carefully.

"Thank you," Stef said. "You're my best friend and there is nobody else in the world I'd rather come home to. No one I'd rather bring the worst parts of myself."

"To me, they're the best parts of you," Jav said. "I know you think it's twisted, but I consider it a goddamn privilege to fuck you back to what you think is the best part of yourself."

The case went horribly on. Sometimes Stef came home and

walked straight into the shower. Other nights he cracked a beer and drank it while staring at the wall. Some nights he was perfectly fine and needed nothing.

Tonight he came home, closed the door, and slid down it to sit on the floor. He patted Roman and stared ten miles away.

Jav, busy at the stove, waited.

All right, what's it gonna be?

A few long inhales and sighs passed, overlaid with the dog's anxious panting and little whines.

"Beer or bourbon?" Jav finally said.

"Bourbon."

Jav poured him a shot of High West Yippee Ki-Yay. Stef bolted it, held the empty glass up for another, and bolted that too. Jav watched, his chest hollowed-out and helpless.

"What do you feel," he said. "Tell me one thing."

Stef drew an enormous breath in. "Sad," he said.

"All right."

"Epic fucking sadness."

Jav crouched down by him. "Yeah."

"Weary," Stef said. "Hopeless. Overwhelmed. Can't find the good in the world. I fucking hurt. I hate everybody and everything." He glanced up. "Except you."

Jav smiled, rolled to sit on his butt and scooted closer. "You can hate me if you feel like it."

"I wouldn't know how." He put down the shot glass, picked up Jav's arms and wrapped them around his shoulders. "I barely know how to tell you how twisted I feel."

Jav held him tighter, stroking his hair. "You just did. Now I know and you don't have to say another fucking word."

Stef exhaled roughly, rolling his forehead along Jav's collarbone. "It's so sick."

"No, it's not. It's how you come home."

Stef sniffed, wiped one cheek, then the other on Jav's shirt. "Fuck."

"I intend to. Why don't you go get yourself ready, okay?"

Stef went statue still in his arms. The only part that moved was his mouth, opening and closing around unspoken words. Jav's nerves pricked up, dialed in, sensing something deep, personal, private and beyond vulnerable was poised on the tip of Stef's tongue.

"What?" Jav said as gently as he could. He spread his hands wide, holding Stef against him. "Tell me."

A deep breath in and a long exhale, but no words. Only the sound of an unvoiced need.

"Finch, tell me," Jav said, running his mouth along Stef's head.

"I want you to get me ready," he said, muffled against Jav's chest.

A window shade of revelation cracked up in Jav's mind. "Oh," he said long and slow.

"I mean ..." Stef's fingers clenched in Jav's shirt.

"No, I get it."

He wouldn't lift up his face. "It's just ... If you—"

"Shh," Jav said, holding him tighter now. Holding him with authority. "I understand now. Don't say anything more."

Stef exhaled again and his body softened, almost went limp. "I've never been able to ..."

"Shh. I know."

"I just don't want to—"

"I'll take care of everything. I'll do everything. Just hold still and let me think a minute."

Jav closed his eyes, framing out the evening, finding the story. Settling into the role of making all the decisions. Asking no questions, simply telling Stef what to do. Or doing it himself. Taking charge.

Not to dominate him. Not for power. To take care of him. To take it all out of his hands. For love.

He saved the world today.

Now he needs me to save him.

He needs me.

"Go in the bedroom," he said. "Take these clothes off and put on sweats and a T-shirt. Then come meet me in the bathroom."

Building on that, he followed Stef down the hall, opened a dresser drawer and took out the prescribed clothing. Any possible decision that could be taken out of Stef's hands, he'd take.

He turned on the heat in the bathroom and spread a clean bath sheet on the heated towel rack. He wrinkled his nose at the floor a moment. Typically, both he and Stef just lay on the bathmat to prep, but it seemed cold and harsh tonight. Oh well. He put down more clean towels and rolled up a couple extra for a pillow. He lit the candle on the commode tank and another on the ledge of the tub, making the environment as nice as he could.

He was crouched at the vanity when Stef came in. "Lie down there," he said. "On your side."

He rinsed off Stef's syringe and reassembled it. Ran the water warm and added two drops of Dr. Bronner's. Part of him was still balking, aware of how recently he'd gotten used to doing this to himself. Doing it to someone else seemed to walk the line between intimate and creepy.

Just do it, he thought. *Pretend someone is prepping you and do it the way you'd want it. Don't be impersonal, don't be pervy, don't make jokes, don't make it a big deal. Be gentle, be cool. And be quiet.*

Taking the syringe and a tube of KY, he knelt behind Stef's body. He slid the waistband of Stef's sweats over his top hip, wiggled it out from beneath his bottom hip, then slid them down to his ankles.

"Bend this knee up," he said softly, as he moved the knee himself. "Roll a little toward your stomach. That's it." He wedged another rolled-up towel under Stef's hip so he wouldn't have to hold himself braced. "Just relax now."

He lubed the tip of the syringe and slid it carefully in. He squeezed slow until it was empty, then slowly withdrew it and tossed it into the sink. He pulled Stef's sweats back up, yanked down the now-toasty towel from the rack and spread it over him.

"Just rest there."

He ran hot water over the tip of the syringe, with an almost holy disregard for the bits of fecal matter going down the drain. It wasn't important. And yet all of this was incredibly important. He set the timer on his phone for ten minutes, then sat on the floor.

"You want to talk about anything?"

"No."

"Tell me if you get cold."

He took Stef's feet in his lap and rubbed them one at a time.

"All right," he said when the timer went off. "You take care of that. Put your pants back on and lie down when you're finished."

He put the towel back on the rack to warm and left, shutting the door quietly. He stripped the bed and put on clean sheets. He turned on Stef's meditation playlist and lit the candles on his shrine. Checked both bedside table drawers that both lube and condoms were where he could easily reach them. After he heard the toilet flush, he waited another thirty seconds before going back into the bathroom. He filled up the syringe again and lubed the tip.

This time, Stef rolled on his stomach and rocked back on his knees. Jav took a little more time pulling his pants down. Caught some of the excess lube on his fingertip and ran it in slow circles around Stef's hole before spreading it taut and easing the syringe inside. When he squeezed it, he slipped his hand under Stef's belly and closed fingers around his penis, stroking it harder as he was filled up.

"Need you to fuck me so bad," Stef whispered.

"I know," Jav said. "And I'm going to. So good."

He rolled Stef down on his side again, curled next to him beneath the warm towel and kissed his mouth. Slid hands under his shirt and then down between his legs, caressing and squeezing.

"I love you," Stef said. "I love nobody the way I love you."

"You're my fucking life," Jav said, kissing him. "And I will do anything."

Another ten breathless minutes passed.

"Take care of that now," Jav said. "Then get in the shower. Don't touch yourself. Just wait for me."

Stef did as told. When Jav stepped into the tub, Stef simply stood under the spray, one shoulder in the tiled wall. Arms crossed, eyes closed and waiting. Jav washed his hair, then lathered him up head to toe, kissing him as he rinsed the suds away. He closed Stef's fingers around the hand-held shower head.

"You hold it," he said. "Don't touch yourself. Just use the water. Put your foot up here on the ledge. That's it."

Stef's mouth was hungry in his, sucking on his tongue and making small little moans in his throat. The shower head wobbled and he groaned when Jav slipped a soapy finger into his ass.

"More," he whispered.

Two fingers now, Jav's other hand pinning Stef's free wrist to the wall.

"You're so ready," he said, scissoring his fingers within that tight, smooth grip. "So smooth and hot and clean. I can't wait to fill it up with my come."

"Fuck me, man. Come on. Right now."

"No, not here."

Jav turned off the water, reached for towels and dried both of them off. Then took Stef by the hand and led him into the dark, warm bedroom. Stef didn't wait for instruction, simply toppled onto his elbows at a corner of the mattress and waited while Jav got a condom on.

"Hold still now," Jav said, slicking both of them up and tossing the lube aside. He positioned the head of his cock and slid into Stef's ass.

"Fuck," Stef whispered, back arched, his hamstrings standing out in tight cords.

Jav's hands found Stef's hipbones and pulled him back and down, burying himself in that impossible heat. "You're mine," he said. "Good, bad or twisted. Once you walk into our place, all of it's mine. I know what to do with it."

Stef's fingers curled in the sheets. "Javi."

"They don't get any more of you. Not your best, not your worst. You're home and it all belongs to me now. Say it."

"It's yours."

"Which parts of it?"

"All of it. It all belongs to you."

"Who else can get to you right now?"

"Nobody."

Jav bent and laid his back all along Stef's, sliding arms beneath him. "I love you."

Stef turned his face, eyes closed. "There's no one else I can bring it to," he whispered. "My whole life ... you've been the only one I can tell."

"I'm gonna keep being that only one. Every day. The rest of your life."

"I love you."

"No one will ever know you the way I do."

"No."

Jav straightened up, started fucking his man with a purpose.

"Put your head down now. Spread your legs for me."

"Javi, I ..."

"Do what I tell you. Just hold still and take my cock."

"God, you give it so good."

"You're going to come for me, then I'm going to fill you up with everything I got. All my worst and best. It's going deep inside you. I got so much, you're going to feel it drip out of you all day tomorrow, reminding you who you belong to ..."

"I'm so fucking in love with you."

Jav bent and ran his tongue up the quivering bumps of Stef's spine. "*You are my life.*" At the nape he let his teeth settle gently, inhaling the damp scent of Stef's hair. "And I'll do anything."

PLUMP

JAV'S CELL RUMBLED ON the coffee table. Stef lifted his head off Jav's thigh to glance at it.

"It's Alex."

His tone was the definition of secure matter-of-factness. Still, Jav always felt weird when Alex called him, unable to shake off a need to be the definition of transparent. He reached over Stef's body to hit the speakerphone button and answer in English, "Hey, man."

"Javi?" Alex's voice skittered all over the place, as if the syllables of Jav's name were made of soap.

"Uh, yeah?"

"Dude, you're never gonna believe what just happened."

"What? You're on speaker so watch your language."

"Yes, my ears are fucking fragile," Stef called.

"Oh my God," Alex said. "Dude, I just got off the phone with my brother."

"With Rog?"

"No. My *brother.*"

"Your ... Wait, what?" He pushed Stef to sit up and hitched closer to the coffee table. "What do you mean?"

"I got a call. From Chile. They found my brother."

"Your actual brother?" Stef said.

"My fucking actual brother," Alex cried. "He's alive, man. They found him. He called me."

"Are you fucking *shitting* me?" Jav said. "Where is he?"

"He lives in Seattle."

"With who? I mean, where's he been all this time?"

"He's been with his family. Who he always thought was his family and they always thought he was theirs. Until they did a DNA test for fun a few months ago and found out he wasn't their kid."

"Wait," Stef said. "His parents had no idea he wasn't their biological child?"

"None."

"Then how did they end up with your mother's baby?"

"That seems to be the big mystery. Obviously they were switched at some point but nobody's figured that out yet. But I'm looking at the lab report from the Medical-Legal Institute. My Y-chromosome matches his Y-chromosome and both ours match my father's. He's my brother."

"DNA don't lie," Stef said. "Man, this is incredible."

"I don't have a word for what it is," Jav said. "And I do words."

"Dammit, Javi, you had one job."

"I suck at it. And I'm so fucking happy for you."

"Are you guys going to meet?" Stef asked.

"Oh, hell yeah."

"Holy shit," Jav said. "I may come to the airport just to be a fly on the wall."

"It's gonna be ugly."

"What's his name?"

"Juleón, but he's called Jude."

"Jude is the patron saint of lost causes," Stef said. "Pardon my font of useless information."

"I think this story fits the definition of lost causes."

"How much adrenaline are you coasting on right now?"

"Seriously, I probably won't sleep for a week."

"This is unbelievable, man," Jav said. "I couldn't be happier. I mean it. This is one of the best phone calls I've ever gotten in my life."

"Oh tell me about great phone calls," Alex said, laughing. "Val is still mopping the floor."

"He just called you, like, out of the blue, 'Hey, my name's Jude, I think I'm your brother'?"

"Pretty much. It's late, I'm tired to begin with. He was nervous as hell and for a minute I couldn't grasp what the hell he was *saying*. He said our DNA matched and I was like, 'Okay, so you're a cousin?' And he said, 'No, I think I'm your brother,' and then my brain completely melted. I know you pride yourself on being an idiot, but I think I won Idiot of the Year tonight."

"You. Brother. Me. Ungh?"

"Like that. But add some aggressive sobbing. Val comes running in and she's like, 'Who's dead?' At one point I was crying so bad I dropped the phone. She picked it up and Jude had dropped *his* phone he was such a wreck. His partner picked it up, so he and Val start talking and crying."

Stef glanced at Jav and mouthed, "Partner?"

"Of *course*," Jav mouthed back, before saying aloud, "I'd kill to have been there."

"I can't even ... This is me, not being able to even."

"It's amazing," Stef said, now busy on his phone.

"I gotta tell Deane and Rog," Alex said.

Jav laughed. "Go make more awesome phone calls. So happy for you, man. Keep me posted, I want to hear everything that happens."

"Shit, I need you to write the damn book."

"I do the words. Ungh."

"Hey, Alex," Stef called, "know what a woodcock is?"

A pause. "It's a bird."

"What do you call a group of woodcocks?"

"A plump. Or a fall. Sometimes a rush."

"Son of a bitch," Stef said, tossing the phone aside.

"I told you—you can't stump him," Jav said.

"A plump of woodcocks, what else would you call it?"

"A fist," Stef muttered.

"And on that note, I gotta go," Alex said. "I'll talk to you guys. Los quiero mucho."

"Te quiero, alondra," Jav said.

"Ciao," Stef said.

Jav ended the call. "Holy crap."

"That is fucking amazing."

"I can't believe it."

Stef gave him a playful shove. "I can't believe he called you before he called his daughter."

"I know, right?"

"And hello, his brother is gay?"

"Of course his brother is gay, that makes so much sense."

"They can discuss your plump woodcock"—Stef climbed over his lap, a knee on either side of Jav's legs—"while I enjoy the real thing."

Jav ran hands along Stef's quads. "We were like this the first time you kissed me."

"More like this." He took Jav's arms and pulled them out wide along the back of the couch, pinning him. "Remember?"

"It's coming back to me."

"I'd waited a fucking month, I wasn't about to let you get away."

"Did I say thank you?"

Stef kissed him. "You were busy."

"Did I mention it was one of the best nights of my life?"

"Top five?"

"Definitely."

Now Stef's mouth ran along Jav's throat. "Did I mention I get extremely horny when I'm jealous?"

"You're jealous? What, of Alex?"

"He's obviously still your bitch, so I feel a need to mark my territory." He looked up, grinning. "I kind of have a thing going in my head. Do you mind just playing along?"

"I have tremendous respect for things in heads." Jav shoved him off and stood up. "Let's go. Thing in head. Ass in bedroom."

"You don't want to fool around here? For old time's sake?"

"No." Jav took Stef's wrist and pulled him along. "My thing requires a lot of horizontal space."

JAV MOVED STEF'S HAND away. "No," he whispered. "Touch any part of yourself you want, but not your dick."

"Christ ..." Stef's head fell side to side. His fingertips drew faint circles on his stomach. They skimmed over his ribs and chest. Closed around the ring in his nipple and pulled it a little. Jav leaned and closed his mouth around the other nipple, biting gently, sucking to the rhythm of his fingers on Stef's prostate.

"God," Stef said. "It's so good."

He moaned as Jav took his mouth and fucked him with his fingers.

"You belong to me," Jav whispered, suffused with power.

"I do."

"You ever gonna let anyone else fuck you this way?"

"No one. Ever again."

Jav didn't know why his ferocity didn't stick around. He could growl only a few lewd or commanding things before tenderness crept back in.

"I love you," he said against Stef's pounding heart. "Finch, I'm so in love with you."

"Stop stop stop," Stef whispered, setting a hand on Jav's shoulder. "Hold up."

"You all right?"

"Yeah, I'm just so fucking close and I don't want to come yet."

He licked his lips beneath closed eyes. His pulse beat around Jav's fingers.

"I love you don't move," he said, so beautiful Jav wanted to die. Was dying to tell him, but he stayed still and quiet, letting the feeling collect in his body until it pressed against the back of his eyes and curled warm in his throat.

I love you, he thought, desperate. *All my life, please, just this, never anything again but this.*

"All right," Stef said, eyes still closed. "Take your fingers out slow. Then get a condom. And don't ask me if I'm sure."

Jav laughed soft as he carefully withdrew his fingers, a stab of fresh lust in his chest at how Stef stayed open and quivering for him.

"God, I want to fuck that," he said.

"You're going to."

He rolled the condom down and took the lube Stef passed him.

"Use a lot. Then put some more on me. Good. That's good. Come here now."

"Oh my God."

"You got this. Just go slow."

Jav set the tip of his penis against that yearning hole. His hand slid to hold Stef's knee up and he slowly pushed inside. It was like moving into the heat of an open oven door. A ferociously tiny, fevered kiln, both crackling and smoldering.

"Jesus," he whispered.

"How's that feel?"

"Holy fuck ..."

Stef's arms raised, his hands reached, pulling at Jav. "Come down here now. Lie on me."

He lay down, sliding an arm beneath Stef's back, pulling Stef's leg around him with the other. He put his heartbeat against Stef's. Pressed his stomach against Stef's hard cock. Set their brows together. Looked for everywhere they could fit.

"Good?" he whispered.

"So good," Stef said. "Never had it so good. Never had anyone in me so good this way. Never had it feel like this."

Jav kissed him, pulling his hips back a little and sliding deep, bumping the breath out of Stef's lungs.

"You can go more. Go a little faster."

"Yeah? Like that?"

"Yeah. It's good. I'll tell you if it's not. Fucking take it, Javi. Take me. Put me where you want, hold me however you want and fuck me the way you want. You're not hurting me, I swear. It's good. Yeah. Like that."

"You like that?"

"Christ."

"Like when I fuck you like that?"

"Don't stop."

He did stop. Long enough to withdraw, turn Stef on his stomach and pull him up onto his knees. He fucked into Stef again, transfixed by the ordinary miracle of lovemaking. How the trembling, delicate skin made way for him when he pushed in. How the fine hairs dragged along his slick cock when he pulled out. The inverted wedge of Stef's torso, tattooed with wings and symbols and shapes. Shoulders bulging with muscle but the nape of his neck soft. Eyes closed as if sleeping but mouth parted against the sheets and his teeth bared to the night. Every part of him open and trusting and surrendered.

"You're so beautiful," Jav said, his hands running in long strokes along Stef's spine.

"Baby."

"God, the way you're just stretched around my cock."

"Javier ..."

"I love how you take me."

"It's so fucking easy, man."

"Your body was made just for mine. You were born to take me. Only me. Only I fuck you like this."

The ferocity stuck with him this time, propelling him further down a boulevard of power. Making him pull back, roughly turn Stef over again, gather his wrists in hand and lean down hard on him. "Where the hell were you, huh? Making me wait forty-four years. Married to some chick who didn't know what to do with you."

Stef's smile broke through his gasping breaths. "My bad."

"Yeah. Your bad giving her all this good."

"I kept the best back. It's yours now."

"Goddamn right it is."

"Fuck me again. Don't stop."

He slid back into Stef's body, hot and tight and deep, bumping the air out of both their lungs. The bottom corners of the fitted sheet had come undone, tangling around their writhing legs.

"We're fucking the sheets right off the bed," Jav whispered. "This is the standard going forward. From now on, I fuck you until the sheets come off."

Stef moaned. "I love you like this." His teeth pressed into Jav's shoulder. "Don't stop being like this."

"I didn't know I could be like this."

"I need to come."

"I know, I can feel it."

"Don't stop. Make me come like this."

Jav stepped off the edge of himself. He left behind his name and his history. He wasn't male, wasn't Dominican. No label could touch him. Not gay, straight or bisexual. Not a top or a bottom. The dominant or the submissive. Only human, entirely and completely human, he disappeared into the most elemental of human acts. Driven by the blunt, primal need to be within the being he loved most in the world and leave part of his soul there.

Later, Stef was fucking him and something happened. It clicked. It went. It worked. It did. It was amazing. Jav's body, utterly relaxed under Stef's. Stef moving effortlessly into his ass. Sliding in and out of him in long, gorgeous strokes. No pain. Only an intense, tickling, buzzing pressure deep within. It rubbed at the base Jav's cock, which was sandwiched tight between their stomachs, wrapped up in its own heated friction as Stef moved in him. In him and on him and against him.

"God, baby, I love it," Stef whispered, the bite of his fingernails dragging along Jav's arms. "I want to make you come in pieces, I swear."

Beneath him, Jav was groaning. Howling. Crying he was going to come, he was going to come so bad, he needed to come and would die if he didn't and then he came. More than came, he arrived. Burst forth into his life in a moment nothing more or less than perfect, mindful presentation. A crystalline instant of oneness.

"Jesus Christ, I think I saw the back side of my skull," he whispered.

Stef collapsed down next to him. "I believe my redeemer liveth."

"Holy shit."

"Man, you are the best plump of woodcock I've ever had in my life."

COME BACK

STEF'S EYES FLUTTERED AND slowly opened. The blue irises wobbled side to side before settling on Jav. The corners of his mouth lifted. The fingers in Jav's gave a feeble squeeze.

"It's all right, I'm here," Jav said. "I'm right here, I won't leave."

Stef made a tiny sound in his throat.

"Te amo mucho. Ve a dormir, Pinzón."

Go to sleep, Finch.

Stef's fingers went limp. His eyes closed. Last to go was the smile, one side of his mouth slackening, then the other.

This happened every other hour. Stef opened his eyes. Gave a weak smile—sometimes enough to make his dimple show, most times not—and then a tiny squeeze.

"It's all right, I'm here," Jav said. "I'm right here, I won't leave."

"Hm."

"Te amo. Vale, ve a dormir, Pinzón."

Stef let go. First his hand. Then his eyes. Then the smile.

Every other hour, the same way.

They'd stripped off his silver rings before the surgery and given them to Jav, who put them on, stacking two and three on a finger to accommodate them all. He'd written silly things about starsilver rings being the only thing to keep a mariner's heart beating. He'd written poignant scenes of a half-man half-horse keeping a desperate bedside vigil for his *gelangos*, his one at hand, the one he belonged to.

It was just a story, he thought, twisting Stef's rings on his fingers. *I didn't mean it to come true. It was already true.*

I don't want this story.

Give him back to me.

"You should go home now," a nurse said gently. "Get some rest."

Jav ignored her, deep in the ritual. Convinced he was as vital to the situation as all the tubes, lines, machines and monitors. If he left, if he missed even one cue to play his part and speak his lines, Stef would die.

I am not leaving, I am not letting you out of my sight, I am not letting you slip through my fingers and disappear forever. If you die, you will die in my arms, on my watch.

And then maybe I'll take a long walk to the George Washington Bridge ...

"Javi, you should eat something," Rory said. "Just go downstairs and put something in your stomach, we'll be right here."

"I'm not hungry."

"Darling, you're exhausted," Lilia said.

"Please stop." He forced the words through clenched teeth, hanging onto a shred of decency. He *was* exhausted. And hungry. But he was not moving from this spot.

They'll have to bodily throw me out of here and it won't be dignified. I'll take a few people out with me. I'll leave claw marks on the walls. I have no problem causing a scene. Bring it ...

People came and went. Doctors. Nurses. The mothers. Stavroula. All tried and failed to coax Jav home to take a break.

"Please just leave me alone," he said over and over, hanging onto himself, trying not to explode at any of the kindness.

Leave us alone. This isn't our story.

Only Ari seemed to understand him.

"How'd you even get up here?" Jav asked. "It's only supposed to be family."

Ari's brows drew down, offended as he pointed to his visitor's badge. "I'm the nephew."

"Well ..."

"Stef is my uncle by cohabitation, my late dog's adopted father and I am here, representing our weird family."

"If you've been recruited to talk me into going home, save your breath."

"Please." The offended expression deepened as he held up a backpack. "I brought home to you."

The pack had clean clothes, a phone charger, ear buds and Jav's leather notebook. Plus a box of Mallomars, which Ari put on the bedside table. "These'll help him get better."

"You are the shit," Jav said.

"With all due sympathy, T, you smell like shit." Ari handed over Jav's shaving kit. "Which won't help Stef get better. Go. Scrub and brush."

"You mean a whore's bath?"

Ari rolled his eyes. "I *said* I was sorry about that."

Admitting the constant anxiety had made him a little ripe, Jav went into the room's adjoining bath and did a quick top-and-tails, brushed his teeth and ran wet hands through his hair. He put on deodorant and fresh clothes and felt if not better, at least more human.

Back in the room, Ari had unwrapped an egg and cheese sandwich on the little table and was peeling the lid off a big cup of coffee. "Eat," he said. "I think better when I'm hungry but you don't."

By now, Jav was so famished, the smell of the food made him

nauseous.

"Take a bite," Ari said. "You're no good to anyone passed out on the floor."

Every bite took an eternity to chew and swallow, but Jav got it down. The strong coffee warmed his stomach but instead of acting as a stimulant, it made him woozy. Ari tugged and dragged the recliner close to the bed, carefully moving a monitor over to make room.

"Put your feet up," he said. "If you can't sleep or won't sleep, at least rest your body."

Jav felt a thousand years old as he canted backward into the chair and flipped up the footrest. "Thanks," he said gruffly.

Ari grunted, brisk and businesslike as he opened his messenger bag. "I brought some work. I'll just hang. In case you doze off."

"I love you right now."

"You love me all the time."

"Yeah, but right now it's particularly fierce."

Ari smiled as he opened his laptop. "What are nephews for?"

"You're all the family I got in the world."

Ari turned an imaginary dial in the air. "Lower the volume, please. I'm working."

"Smartass," Jav mumbled. Yawning big, he reached through the bedside rail and held Stef's hand.

Almost time.

Minutes ticked by in beeps and buzzes. Jav waited, one socked foot jiggling on the rest.

Getting to be time. Should be soon.

Anytime now, Finch.

Don't you do this. Don't you fucking dare, I will kill y—

Stef's eyes fluttered and opened.

Relief prickling up and down his limbs, Jav hitched forward a little to get in sight. "Hey."

Stef smiled. The dimple showed this time. His hand squeezed.

"It's all right, I'm here," Jav said. "I'm right here, I won't leave."

"Hm."

"It's all right. Go to sleep, Finch."

The bare fingers softened. Stef shut his eyes and the smile faded. He looked so small.

Jav exhaled and melted back into the chair. His stomach was full and the tank was empty. He fought off wave after wave of fatigue that made his chin drop and jerk back up.

"T, you're gonna break your neck," Ari said quietly. "Vale, cierra tus ojos."

Close your eyes.

"I can't," Jav said.

"Come on, twenty-minute power nap. I'll be right here, I promise. On the truth of my blood."

"Don't quote me."

"Said no author ever."

With a last worried glance at Stef, and another reassuring glance at Ari, Jav gave in and let the dark behind his closed eyelids take him away.

You are my greatest story. And I love nothing the way I love you.

Don't quote me.

I didn't write it to come true.

Take my secrets, take my treasures, take my words and my soul. Take me into your merciful heart and take everything I have.

Just give him back to me.

Give him back.

Give him ...

He woke with a jolt, disoriented. While he slept, someone had rolled the recliner away from the bed. He hadn't felt a thing. Ari was gone. A tall man with thick, white hair sat next to the sleeping

Stef. He had a book in his lap and was reading out loud.

"*In pairs they galloped by, and though every now and then one rose in his stirrups and gazed ahead and to either side, they appeared not to perceive the three strangers sitting silently and watching them. The host had almost passed when suddenly Aragorn stood up and called in a loud voice—*"

Jav finished the passage: "'*What news from the North, Riders of Rohan?*'"

Marcus Finch looked back and closed *The Two Towers* around his finger. "You're awake."

"Barely." Jav put the recliner's footrest down. "What year is it?"

"Twenty fifty-three. I'm a holographic image from the afterlife."

Jav smiled at Stef's joke coming from his father's mouth. "You come straight from the airport?"

"Yes."

"Flight was okay?"

"Could've been better."

They looked at each other expectantly. Jav had only met Marcus once before, when he and Stef went to Germany last summer. It was a perfectly pleasant visit, but not long enough to move past stiff cordiality. Jav still wasn't quite sure where he stood with Marcus. Or where Marcus stood with his son living with another man. Whether he'd reached acceptance with Stef's sexuality, or was still disappointed and bewildered by it.

Right now, Jav didn't give a shit. He was too tired. Too upset. Too freaked out and terrified to give one flying fuck if Marcus approved of him or not. He moved closer to the bed, smoothed a sheet that didn't need smoothing, straightened the box of Mallomars on the side table. Fussing and re-arranging for no other reason than to assert his entitled presence.

Why not whip it out and pee a circle around the bed? That'll show him.

"They told me you've been here three straight days," Marcus said.

"Mm."

"You must be wiped out."

"I'm all right."

Marcus's eyes were lighter than Stef's cobalt ones. Piercing under thick brows. But kind. "We didn't get to talk much while you were in Germany."

Jav shook his head. He took a little fold of Stef's hospital gown and rubbed it between his fingers.

"Sit down, Javi," Marcus said. Like his eyes, the tone was light, kind, but piercing.

Jav sat.

Marcus set *The Two Towers* aside and rubbed his palms together. "Using Javi might've been too familiar. Sorry. I don't know if I've earned that yet."

"It's fine."

"We don't know much about each other, do we?"

Jav raised his eyebrows.

"I suspect we know the significant things. You probably know I behaved badly when Stef came out. I know you've been on your own a long time. You left home at nineteen?"

"Seventeen."

"Just after your father died."

"That's right."

Marcus hesitated. "Stef told me your father was your one and only champion during a bad time."

"I was outed before I even knew I was in. A lot of people behaved badly, but everything happened too fast and too harshly for me to process."

"I see."

"My dad was disappointed in me," Jav said slowly. "But he had my back. He believed in second chances. The real abuse didn't start until after he died."

"And then it was over. For good. You were out and on your own. You've been taking care of yourself ever since."

Jav nodded.

"Again," Marcus said, "you must be wiped out."

Tired and sad to his bones, Jav looked away.

"It wouldn't be a surprise to learn you've trusted nobody since." Marcus reached and put a hand on Stef's leg. "Except for this guy."

"This for that," Jav murmured.

"Pardon?"

"This for that. Most of my life has been transactional. I never trusted that people offered me a *this* without expecting a *that* in return. Instead of appreciating kindness, I looked at it as suspect. It always had a price. A catch. Even if it didn't, I attached one. Just to be safe."

"I get it."

"Do you?"

Marcus sat back. "This may surprise you but I do know a little something about changing behavior patterns at an advanced age."

Jav had to smile then. "Punto. As my dad would say."

"What's it say on your badge?"

"My badge?" Jav looked down at the visitor's sticker on his shirt.

"Under your name, what does it say?"

"Family."

"Yes, it does." Marcus leaned forward and put an arm on the bedrail. "I'm talking to you as family. All right? And as family, I want you to go home and eat something. Get in bed and get a few hours of sleep. Because right now, you're the one thing keeping Stef going. Which is why I need you to eat and rest. Will you do that for me?"

Jav said nothing.

"I read *Trueblood*," Marcus said. "Twice, actually."

"Yeah?"

"For a fatherless child, you grasped fatherhood in a way that touched me. I don't mean that in a sentimental way. I mean it got under my skin. How you made Da the most giant of giantwords and gave it a dual meaning. Father and the courage to be a father. It was really something."

"Thank you," Jav said, his defenses up again because hell if he'd be *flattered* into leaving.

"I'm not your father," Marcus said. "But I'm speaking to you as one. I'm not feeling any of that steel-hearted courage right now. Stef needs you. And I need you. Please go home a few hours and rest. Because frankly, nobody's going to get through this without you."

Jav closed his eyes. Still averse to the idea, but listening to why it could be a good one.

"If anything alarming happens, I will call you," Marcus said. "Immediately. You have my word."

Jav drew in a tremendous breath and held it. "Is this where I get to ask for something in return?"

"If you need to."

"He wakes up a little. Every hour or so. Opens his eyes. Every time it happens, I tell him I'm right here and I won't leave. Then he goes back to sleep." He looked at Marcus then. "When it happens again, you tell him I'll be right back."

"I will."

Jav exhaled. "All right." He planted his hands on his knees and stood up. He looked around for a jacket but he didn't have one. He came here three days ago with just his wallet, keys and phone. He had nothing to collect to delay his leaving. He just had to go.

I choose to go, he thought, walking on stiff legs to the door. *I am doing a favor for a father. Out of the kindness of my merciful heart.*

His hand was on the knob when Marcus called to him.

"Javier."

Jav turned back. From Stef's bedside, Marcus stared at him. A long, assessing gaze that weighed and measured. His hand lifted. A finger pointed.

Then he smiled and said, "Come back with a ring."

Jav blinked. He glanced down at his silver-clad fingers, then up again, not understanding.

Marcus's gaze twinkled now. "Come back with a ring and we'll discuss your intentions with my son."

Jav's heart turned over and the edges of his eyes blurred wet. Happiness swirled with an intense grief and poured down the back of his throat. Acceptance strengthened his spine even as his body shook with the need to go running to someone in authority, to a wise, kind advocate, an old friend, a mentor.

He'd never wanted so badly to have his father back.

Marcus's pointing finger retreated and he picked up Tolkien again. "Go rest now, Javi."

Do you understand? Answer your commander.

Jav clutched the doorknob hard, his voice hoarse as he answered, "Yes, sir."

Guys, I swear, I'm not pulling a Trueblood here. Jav comes back with a ring and Stef's going to be all right. Promise. —SLQR

BAJA LA CABEZA

STEF OPENED THE DOOR with a big smile. He looked great. Shaved and sharp, hair damp, leather jacket on. Still a little gaunt in the face but his eyes were popping blue and bright and he hugged Ari in a laughing, exuberant embrace. He was dying to get out of the apartment.

Jav was subdued by comparison. His hug was a sigh. Always so meticulously clothed and groomed, his jeans bagged in the ass and his scruffy cheek scraped Ari's face. His eyes were shadowed and even his smile was tired. As if Stef turning a corner made Jav downshift.

Walking along the High Line, Stef was full of conversation and appreciation for the day. He and Jav held hands. He kept saying how good it felt to be out. He stopped to take a picture of the river, then pulled Jav and Ari in for a selfie which he put on Instagram.

After the impromptu hospital wedding went viral on social media, Jav's fans had become Stef's fans. The Finch went from hot husband to hashtag. Flowers piled up outside Cushman Row. An unsolicited GoFundMe raised fifty thousand dollars for the couple, which they donated to charity. The video post of Stef coming home from the hospital got nearly half a million views.

"When do they think you can go back to work?" Ari asked, as

they passed the Exodus Project warehouse building.

Stef looked up wistfully at the windows of the CCT art room. "Maybe another month or so."

"You miss it?"

"Yeah." Stef rubbed his chin, brows furrowed. "I do."

"You can't even do some part-time work?"

Stef smiled. "No, because right now, all my clients want to talk about me and how I'm doing. I'll have to transition back in carefully. Still not sure how I'm going to do it."

He made to walk off but Jav put a hand on his arm. "Hold up," he said, his other thumb dancing over his phone.

Ari squinted at the warehouse, with a feeling what was happening. Sure enough, the tall windows of the art room cranked open on their hinges and a dozen men and women leaned out, waving.

"Finch," they called.

"My man."

"You look beautiful, baby."

"Love you."

Stef laughed deep in his belly and chest, waving both arms and catching the blown kisses.

Both his pace and his mood slowed down as they neared Hudson Yards. He had a little headache but damn, the fresh air felt good. Sure, he could eat. At the pub, he drank half his beer and let Ari finish his sandwich. He grew quieter, rubbing more and more at his temples. He got a little misty when one of Jav's readers came by the table, apologized for interrupting but wanted to say how wonderful it was to see him out and about.

"People are unbelievably kind," Stef said afterward. "I still can't get over it. Them knowing who I am, I mean."

"Mi fama es su fama," Jav said.

Stef dipped a fry in ketchup, took a small bite and put it back down on the plate. He felt fine, just not hungry. He could manage the walk back home, no problem. What a day. This was great. He leaned on Jav's shoulder and sighed. Jav ran his mouth across the top of Stef's head, matching the sigh.

Ari's uncles had never been particularly demonstrative in his presence. He always got the sense they deliberately refrained from being physically affectionate in front of him, but he didn't know how to tell them they didn't need to cool it for his sake. But since getting married, Jav and Stef were out of fucks for anyone's sake. They leaned all over each other, touched, hugged and kissed without a shit between them to give.

"God, would you two cool it already?" Ari said, then ducked the fry Stef threw at his head.

Outside, the cloud cover had broken and Stef screwed up his eyes in the bright sun. Jav took off his shades, handed them over and then hailed a cab. Stef didn't object. He slid inside and hunched within his jacket.

"Did it get cold all of a sudden?" he said, blowing on his hands. The moons of his fingernails had a bluish hue.

"Here, hon," Jav said, pulling gloves out of his pocket. "Zip up your jacket."

By the time they got home, Stef was wearing Jav's gloves and Ari's ball cap, yet he was shivering as they walked into the apartment.

"Damn, I got chilled off," he said. "I'm going to jump in the shower."

"I thought I'd make soup," Jav said. "It can sit on the back burner and we can eat it whenever."

"Sounds good."

The bathroom door closed. Jav started clattering around the kitchen.

"Need help?" Ari said.

"No."

He pushed at the terse tone. "You okay?"

"I'm fine, I just want to be alone in my head and cook with nobody talking to me." He smiled at Ari. "You're family, I can say shit like that."

Ari patted him. "Tu mierda es mi mierda."

"God, where in the hell did you pick up that accent?"

"What are you talking about?"

"You sound Argentinian."

"I was dating a girl from Buenos Aires few months ago."

"She sure rubbed off on you."

"That's what she said."

Jav swatted him. "Get out of my kitchen."

Ari flopped on the couch, opened his laptop and pounded out some emails. The background noises wove together in a domestic hum. The rhythmic chop of a knife on wood. The sizzle of oil in a skillet and the low roar of the kitchen fan. An odd lull made Ari look up. Jav stood still by the fridge, a hand on the handle, staring into space.

"You all right, T?" Ari called.

"Hm?"

"When you go into a trance like that, you're either tired or you're getting an idea."

A beat. "I'm tired."

"No ideas?"

"Not many lately. But they'll come back."

"No doubt. The compass never worries."

"Please don't quote me," Jav said. "Said no author ever."

Fridge opening and closing. Running water. Pots and pans. Ari's fingers danced on the keyboard.

A noise that didn't belong.

What was that?

Ari tilted his head, fingers poised. Blinked twice. Then started typing again.

Jav gathered up the garbage bag and took it out.

"Jav?"

Ari stopped typing. He twisted to look back toward the bathroom. The water wasn't running anymore and through the door, Stef was calling. Just the tiniest edge of need in his voice. *That* was the sound that didn't belong.

Ari put his laptop aside and hopped over the back of the couch.

"Javi?" The voice rose, its edge grew keener.

Ari rattled knuckles on the door. "Stef, you okay?"

"Yeah. Could you tell Jav to come in a sec?"

"Hold on, he took the garbage out." Ari touched the doorknob. It wouldn't be locked. He knew Stef had passed out in the bathroom a couple weeks ago. Jav kicked the locked door in to get to him and afterward, laid down an ironclad rule that doors could be closed between him and Stef, but not locked. Ever.

But Ari wasn't Jav. "Do you need help?" he called.

"I'm okay," Stef said, a little too cheerfully, as if reassuring himself. "Just tell him to—"

Jav brushed past Ari and briskly opened the door. "I'm right here, babe, what's up?" All his subdued fatigue had dropped away like a discarded jacket. His manner crisp, commanding and unflappable.

"I got a little light-headed," Stef said.

"Okay, stay there. I'll help you out."

"I still have soap on me."

"No worries. Ari, querido, turn the stove down?"

Heart thumping, Ari turned the burner to low and switched off the fan. He sat at the island, eyes closed, listening to the voices from the open bathroom door. Muffled through the shower spray before it turned off again.

"Wait, wait," Jav said. "The floor's wet. Give me your foot, let me dry it off so you don't slide. Now step over. Lean on my shoulder. Good. Give me the other foot now."

"So weird," Stef said. "One minute I was fine, the next I like ... hit the wall."

"How's the headache?"

"Getting worse."

"The usual? Behind your eyes?"

"Yeah. Kind of pinching the bridge of my nose."

"Your teeth are chattering now. Go on, get dressed. Need help?"

"No, I'm okay."

"Go slow."

Stef walked on his own to the bedroom, one towel around his waist, another around his shoulders.

"Dry your head," Jav called. The thwack of a bathmat shook out, the rattle of shower curtain rings across the rod. Then he crossed into the bedroom. "You still dizzy?"

"No, but I'm wiped out. What the fuck?"

"You took a long walk, got a little sun and a lot of cold air, then you had half a beer. That's pretty much the fuck."

"God, I'm a pussy."

"You want to get in bed?"

"No, I'll go on the couch."

"Get in bed if you want."

"What I want is to be near you. Shit, do I feel hot?"

"Come here. Yeah, you might be running a fever. Thermometer's in your bedside drawer, check and see."

Jav went back in the kitchen, mumbling in Spanish under his breath. Stef came out, fleece zipped to his chin, frowning at the digital thermometer. "It's beeping but I don't know what it's saying."

"Give it," Jav said. "You have to hold this button and wait until it flashes. Now put it in your ear. Hold still."

Watching his uncle put a hand on Stef's head, and with the other hold a thermometer in his ear, Ari's throat grew warm. The moment was so ordinarily tender, so mundanely intimate, yet he felt like he was spying on them having sex. He was filled with affection for the two men, and a fascinated, bone-deep, lonely envy at the same time.

Who would take care of me like that?

Three sharp beeps and Jav looked at the display. "Yeah, one hundred point one. You got a low-grade going. Take two Tylenol."

Stef settled on the couch, pulling the knitted blanket over his legs. He opened a book but within ten minutes, it was face-down on his chest and his eyes were closed. Ari reached and clicked off the standing lamp, then pulled the blanket up higher. The corners of Stef's mouth twitched. "Thanks, kiddo," he whispered.

Ari patted him. "Just rest."

He reached for his laptop again, then stopped, gaze narrowing on the kitchen. His uncle stood with his hands braced on the countertop. Not staring into space but down into the sink. Breathing slowly in and out. As if the air were a knife and he was trying to ease it into his lungs.

Ari got up, moving on careful, socked feet. He rubbed a tentative circle between Jav's quivering shoulder blades. "Hey, Tío."

"I'm okay."

"Vamos a superarlo."

"I know," Jav said. "It's just hard."

Ari slid his hand and squeezed the back of Jav's neck. "You're amazing to him. How you take care without taking over."

Jav gave half a laugh and his shoulders flicked. "That's the hardest part. Not hovering and anticipating every little thing.

Letting go and trusting he'll ask for help, but knowing when he's too proud to."

"No one knows him like you."

"Por supuesto. I'm fine when he runs a fever or gets light-headed in the shower, but when he leaves half his lunch on his plate, it just fucking kills me."

"See?" Ari said. "I can only hope I find someone who knows me down to the last bite of a sandwich. Someone who loves me the way you love him."

Jav nodded, then his head dropped and stayed there for another ferocious sigh. "You will."

Then you'll know, was the unspoken subtext.

Ari slid both arms around his uncle and squeezed hard. Jav held onto his forearms. He wasn't crying, but Ari could feel him shaking.

"You're doing great," Ari said, awed and humbled by the love in this house.

"Thanks." A chuckle. "Worry about everything, panic about nothing."

"Go lie down with him, okay? Close your eyes a while."

"Yeah, maybe I ..."

"You need to rest. I'm family so I can say shit like this."

Jav turned and hugged him, ruffling Ari's hair. "Te quiero."

"Baja la cabeza. Put your head down."

Jav seemed grateful for someone telling him what to do. He heeled off his sneakers and lay on the couch's long side. Stef roused enough to scootch down and pass a pillow, then they lay with their heads perpendicular in the corner. Stef's crown against Jav's chest. Jav's arm draped across and their fingers linked. The thick silver of their rings peeking between. Friends, lovers, mates and husbands.

Truebloods, Ari thought. He draped a second blanket over Jav.

Then pulled his sketchbook from his messenger bag, found a pencil and rubber eraser on Stef's art desk. He settled on a kitchen stool and began to sketch his uncles.

STARDUST

"ANY OTHER QUESTIONS FOR ME?" Dr. Park asked.

"No," Jav said.

"Yes," Stef said. "Any reason we can't have sex?"

"Absolutely none," Park said, scribbling some last notes. "Anything that releases endorphins, promotes well-being, reaffirms your relationship and induces a good night's sleep, we highly encourage."

"Highly," Stef said, glancing at Jav. "*And* the royal we."

Park looked up. "Were you worried?" she asked Jav gently.

"No."

"Yes," Stef said.

Jav crossed his arms. "I'm just cautious."

Park smiled, gathering her papers and squaring the edges. "The only restriction is how you feel. You can be cautious and be lovers. You don't need my sign-off or green light but if it matters, you have it. Go to bed. Enjoy."

"YOU WANT TO EAT SOMETHING?" Jav said, closing his laptop.

"Your ass."

Jav froze mid-stretch, tilted back in his chair. "Pardon?"

"You heard me. Start prepping my dinner."

He laughed, but stopped as Stef stared him down over the tops of his glasses. "I don't hear any running water, Landes."

Jav's eyes swiveled toward the bathroom then back at Stef. One side of his mouth smiled. "You sure y—"

"Yes," Stef said. "I want my boyfriend tonight. Not my worried husband or my devoted caretaker. You know?"

Jav nodded, sighing. "I know. I want it, too."

"So go. Have a drink, get high, take a bath. Do whatever you gotta do and let's freakin' get laid."

The front chair legs came down with a bang and Jav stood up. "Challenge accepted."

Stef flipped the paper back up with a crisp thwack. "Scrub your ass good."

"Back off, bitch, I wiped your ass *immaculate* in the hospital."

The bathroom door slammed.

"Yes, you did," Stef said softly.

He picked up clothes and shoes from the bedroom floor, pulled the comforter and pillows straight, turned off all the lamps except the small one on his shrine. He waited until all the flushing was over and the water in the bath turned off, then grabbed the bottle of Appleton Estate and two lowball glasses. On impulse, he tucked Jav's new copy of Neil Gaiman's *Stardust* under his elbow.

"Room service," he called.

"It's open."

The bathroom was steamy and dark, a lit candle on the edge of the sink. Jav lolled in the tub, his hair slicked back. Stef brought in more candles and poured out two shots of rum to chug, then more generous tots to sip. He sat on the bathmat and read out loud. Jav rested an arm on the ledge of the tub, cheek on his bicep, damp fingers playing with a fold of Stef's shirt. The walls of the little room drew close. Even the fixtures seemed to lean on their elbows and listen.

"This is nice," Jav said softly, drawing up Stef's neck and behind his ear.

Stef smiled, perfectly comfortable and happy and not wanting to jostle the moment with extra words.

Jav closed his eyes. "I'm buzzed."

"Good."

He opened his eyes and they stared a long moment. Jav's hand curled around the back of Stef's head and drew him close.

"C'mere," he whispered before their mouths touched.

Stef closed his eyes now. Still holding the book, he let Jav kiss him. Nudge his lips apart and taste him. Sweet with rum, sharper in the breath exhaling into the back of Stef's throat.

"Give me your tongue," Jav said.

Stef followed Jav back into his mouth. Sighed as Jav's other wet hand undid a button and slid under his shirt, stroking his chest, his palm making circles on Stef's heart. Expert fingers closed around the ring in his nipple, the perfect amount of pinch and just a little tug, the *slightest* twist. Not too hard. Just enough to turn him on and want more. Jav got it right every single time.

The book tumbled from Stef's fingers. The hand in his hair tightened. He turned further into the kiss, sliding his palm around the back of Jav's neck.

"I miss you, baby," Jav said.

"I miss you too." Rolling up and onto his knees and pressing Jav back into the tub, nestling his head down on the ledge. His other hand found Jav's penis, hard under the soft water. Jav groaned in his mouth, his knees and his kiss opening wider.

"That misses you too," he said.

"I can tell." Stef's hand slid. Jav's balls were warm and relaxed in his hand. Beneath them, the softest, most secret skin. He slid a fingertip against his hole and rubbed gently. "Does this miss me?"

"Yeah." Jav's knees fell until they pressed the sides of the tub.

Stef closed teeth around Jav's bottom lip and tugged a little. Let go and licked his upper lip. "I'm going to fuck you so hard and fill you up so good tonight."

Jav's hips bucked a little, his pelvis chasing after Stef's roving fingertip. "Give it."

"I will."

"Now."

"Dry off and get in bed," Stef said.

Jav's laugh had an edge of agony. "You're killing me."

"Go on. I'll be there in a minute. Don't touch yourself, just wait for me."

He drained the tub and took a quick shower. When he emerged, Jav had moved some of the candles into the bedroom and put on Stef's meditation playlist. He lay on his stomach in the center of the bed, gorgeous and naked, lined in gold light.

Stef slid on top of him. "I feel really good right now."

"So do I."

"I don't want to talk too much. I don't want you to ask if I'm okay. If I'm not, I'll say so."

Jav exhaled. "Turning off the caretaker part of my head is harder than I thought."

"Then don't turn it off," Stef said. "Just turn on the boyfriend switch, too. Be both."

"All right."

"You give so much all day long. Now let me give."

The corners of Jav's closed eyes crinkled. "Stop talking."

Stef took his time, rubbing Jav's back and limbs, kissing him everywhere. Still, he knew his husband at a cellular level. Jav was relaxed, but not quite surrendered to the night. He had a mental foot on the floor and one eye open, checking in that Stef was all right.

Stef lay flat on Jav's back and squeezed him. "I love you so fucking much."

Jav's fingers twined with his. "I wish I could get out of my head," he whispered.

"Then you wouldn't be you," Stef said.

Jav's back expanded and contracted in a sigh. "I love your hands on me."

"I love your body. I'll never look at you and not get turned on."

"Even when I'm being a moron?"

"Even then. You don't know what kind of strength I draw from touching you. It grounds me. I can get through anything as long as I can get my hands on you."

"I can handle whatever if I can handle you."

"Don't show off."

Jav smiled over his shoulder. "Speaking of showing off, I recall someone promised ass eating?"

Stef moved back on his knees. "Put your weird head down, Landes."

He kissed down Jav's spine. Slid his thumbs along the crack of Jav's ass, spread him open and licked slowly. Jav shivered, calves twitching on either side of Stef's body. Stef curled hands around Jav's hip bones and pulled him up and back onto his knees. Jav stuffed the pillows under his chest and when he was settled, he reached his arms behind him, wrists crossed in the small of his back.

"Take them," he murmured. "I'm still trying to hold onto everything. Take it out of my hands."

Stef curled a hand around his wrists, pinning them. He wormed a knee between Jav's feet. "Spread your legs for me," he said. "More."

He ran his free hand over and around Jav's ass, let him be open and vulnerable on his knees, exposed from stem to stern. Waiting. And wanting.

"Lick me," Jav finally whispered.

"I will."

"Now."

"Shh."

"Please."

"Hold still, honey."

He felt Jav's engine rev up a gear. The night pulled until it stretched translucent from wall to trembling wall. Stef moved between Jav's legs, where every fine hair on his quads was sitting up and begging. His erection pressed against the pillows, pointing down and already leaking. Stef licked it away, then let his tongue trail up the shaft, over the seam of Jav's balls, up into the crack, over his hole and finally to the small of his back where he sucked on Jav's fingers.

"Fuck," Jav whispered.

"Oh, I will."

"Do that again."

Stef did.

"Do it forever."

He licked Jav everywhere. Got him good and wet with his mouth, then reached for lube and started using his fingers. He let go of Jav's wrists so he could grip his cock, and Jav obediently kept his hands behind his back. Fingers reaching and straining as if still confined. He was out of his head and into a story now.

"You're so ready for me," Stef said, three fingers deep and the palm of his other hand damp with pre-come.

"Finch, you need to fuck me yesterday."

Stef eased his fingers out and made to reach for a condom.

"Don't," Jav said. "Not tonight. I don't want anything between us tonight."

They didn't often fuck bareback. Only on their special-est occasions or in their most dire moments. Tonight had a unique edge of desperation and Stef took his time breaching that molten, squeezing heat. He fucked into Jav an inch at a time, watching his lover go from a clenched fist to an open palm.

"So good," Jav said. "So good when I feel it going in me like that."

Mindful that Jav had finally stepped off the edge of his daily worries, Stef kept an eye on himself. Topping was strenuous work and his body was already in a weak place. Soon his back began to spasm and his knees trembled with more than desire. Within the raging passion, he was getting physically tired. He needed to get off his legs if he wanted this to last.

"Come finish like this," he said, slipping free and crawling toward the headboard. "Come here." He piled up the pillows and reclined against them. "Turn around now."

Jav pivoted on his knees, showing his beautiful back, with the charm of goldfinches flying around Trueblood's coordinates. He knelt between Stef's legs, tucked his feet under Stef's butt and slowly canted his hips into Stef's lap.

"Hold me open," he said, guiding Stef's cock.

Stef held his cheeks apart, watching as just the tip of his cock disappeared, stretching Jav wide. They both exhaled together, feeling Jav's pulse beat through the tight warmth.

"Baby," Stef whispered. "That's so fucking beautiful. The shape you make around me."

"I want this forever."

"I will never not want you, I swear." Stef drew one of Jav's wrists back, then the other. Pulled on him a little as he resisted the urge to push. Jav leaned off-balance, hanging by his arms, and sank down, taking Stef the rest of the way.

"That's it," Stef said. "Christ, you are so fucking tight."

"God," Jav cried, his voice strangled and hoarse. He leaned more, the angle pulling Stef's cock down low. "You're all up in me."

He clenched down hard and Stef's balls tightened, ready to fire. Orgasm spread its wings, poised on the edge. He set his teeth and tried to hold it back, but his body was tired. Three shots of rum on an empty stomach wasn't helping his self-control. Part of him wanted to time it right and come together with Jav, the other part just wanted to blow.

"Javi, it's close," he said through his locked jaw.

"Me too. Almost." Jav rose up a little, rocked his hole around the tip of Stef's cock. Then he took him all the way in again and Stef came fast, yelling his head off and pumping hot into Jav's body, bucking and writhing. Fingernails digging into Jav's forearms as he yanked him down harder.

"Easy, easy," Jav said, checking Stef's wild thrusts.

"God ..."

"Don't move anymore, baby. Hold still."

"Sorry."

"It's okay."

"Did you come?"

"No, I missed. Hold still now."

"Holy shit."

Jav laughed softly. "Jesus, that was a huge fucking load."

"I know," Stef said, sucking wind. "I wanted to wait for you. I totally fucking lost it."

"It's all right, let go of me. Give me my hands back." Jav leaned on his palms, shivering one last time before carefully easing Stef out of him. He turned over, rested his legs over Stef's and scooted in close.

"Finish me off," he said, pouring lube into Stef's palm. "God, I'm so fucking hard it hurts."

He leaned back on the heels of his hands, knees splayed, his engorged penis like granite in Stef's hand. Skin like bronze in the candlelight. Glowing with sweat and frustration.

"You're so hot," Stef said, getting his thumb on the sweet spot and his other hand scooping up Jav's balls and squeezing. "Fucking love this cock."

Jav fell further onto his elbows, raising his hips. "Go back in my ass," he whispered. "Rub it out of me from inside."

He was still stretched open and slick with Stef's come. Two fingers slipped through his hole like nothing. Stef curled them up and in and found Jav's prostate, started rubbing in the circular rhythm he knew Jav loved.

"Yeah," Jav moaned, a hand sliding around his chest and stomach before careening down to cup his balls, pulling on them, wanton and uninhibited. "Yeah, like that. Like that, Stef. Like that, do it like that I'm gonna come so bad ..."

The babble disintegrated as he shot, head thrown back and teeth bared to the night. Spurting as far as his collarbones, howling in his throat as Stef squeezed the last drops out of him. He collapsed on his back, belly and chest heaving, forearms crossed over his face.

"God," he gasped, muffled. "Nobody fucks me like you."

"Nobody." Stef stroked him one last time, then stilled his hand to a gentle grip, knowing Jav went from turned-on to ticklish in about six seconds.

Jav's panting turned to laughter. "That was so good, man."

Stef reached for the bath towel on the floor and wiped them up. Then Jav pivoted around and rolled over, lying with his head on Stef's chest. "Jesus, I needed that."

"Yeah."

"I mean, I needed you to fuck me. But I didn't know how bad until it was happening."

"Me too," Stef said against his temple. "You carry so much for the both of us. I just wanted you to put it all down tonight."

"Took a while to get out of my head but then when I gave you my hands, something clicked." He burrowed closer, arms winding around Stef's body. "It made me remember. Or forget. Or ... something." A shiver went across his shoulders.

Stef rubbed his back. "Cold?"

"Little."

He pulled up the covers around them. Waited for Jav to ask if he was all right.

Jav didn't. "I love you so much, I'm going to kill you."

Stef smiled and brought their twined fingers to his mouth, closed his eyes and breathed. "You're my life. Do I tell you that enough?"

"You do, but I'll always love hearing it."

After a few minutes, Jav got up to pee and came back with *Stardust.* He lay down between Stef's legs again, resting on his chest. "Read again?"

"Sure." He tucked the covers around them. "Is this comfortable?"

"It's perfect." Jav put his head down. "Just keep holding me."

"I got you."

"The candles–"

"Shh. I'll take care of everything tonight."

He balanced the book on Jav's shoulder blades and read out loud.

The music looped. The flames flickered in pools of melted wax.

Jav fell asleep in his arms, limp and sated and selfish.

Stef had never loved him more.

ABOUT THE AUTHOR

A FORMER PROFESSIONAL DANCER AND TEACHER, Suanne Laqueur went from choreographing music to choreographing words. Her work has been described as therapy fiction, emotionally intelligent romance and contemporary train wreck.

Laqueur's novel *An Exaltation of Larks* was the Grand Prize winner in the 2017 Writer's Digest Awards and won first place in the 2019 North Street Book Prize. Her debut novel *The Man I Love* won a gold medal in the 2015 Readers' Favorite Book Awards and was named Best Debut in the Feathered Quill Book Awards. Her follow-up novel, *Give Me Your Answer True*, was also a gold medal winner at the 2016 RFBA.

Laqueur graduated from Alfred University with a double major in dance and theater. She taught at the Carol Bierman School of Ballet Arts in Croton-on-Hudson for ten years. An avid reader, cook and gardener, she started her blog EatsReadsThinks in 2010.

Suanne lives in Westchester County, New York with her husband and two children.

Visit her at suannelaqueurwrites.com

All feels welcome. And she always has coffee.

ALSO BY SUANNE LAQUEUR

THE FISH TALES
The Man I Love
Give Me Your Answer True
Here to Stay
The Ones That Got Away

VENERY
An Exaltation of Larks
A Charm of Finches
A Scarcity of Condors
The Voyages of Trueblood Cay
Tales from Cushman Row
A Plump of Woodcocks

SHORT STORIES
Love & Bravery
An Evening at the Hotel

GIVEAWAY
Enter to win a signed copy of An Exaltation of Larks
All entrants receive a free ebook of The Man I Love
http://lqrwrites.com/freebook

www.ingramcontent.com/pod-product-compliance
Lightning Source LLC
Chambersburg PA
CBHW070913100726
47907CB00008B/2302